CONVULSIVE

(New museums birth atrocity in every flex)

Apocalypse Party

Design by Mike Corrao
Cover by Matthew Revert

Paperback: 978-1-954899-05-6

Printed in the United States of America

FIRST AMERICAN EDITION

9 8 7 6 5 4 3 2 1

CONVULSIVE

Joe Koch

Introduction

There's something to be said of a writer with an exceptional dexterity when it comes to language, an expert prowess when it concerns crafting beguiling and truly visceral text that will mystify and astound even the most temperamental of readers. Joe Koch is indeed a writer with such a gift—an immense talent when it comes to language that spellbinds, enchants, and bewilders the reader until they are transformed. Their work is magnetic, transformative, and alluring while simultaneously serving as something especially grotesque.

I first encountered Koch's exquisite writing when I first purchased a copy of their iconic novella, *The Wingspan of Severed Hands*, published by Weirdpunk Books. At the time, I had recently been signed on to Weirdpunk to release my own novella, *Things Have Gotten Worse Since We Last Spoke*, and I had heard such wonderful things of Koch's literary competency that I knew I was in for such a treat. Moreover, I was especially smitten with the idea of reading Koch's writing seeing as they had received praise from one of my greatest writing influences, Dennis Cooper. Naturally, I expected their writing to operate at a certain level when I first picked up my copy and started to read; however, I could have never anticipated the skill with which Koch controls their prose—deeply visceral and mesmeric. Unrestrained from conventional form and instead freely reveling in the poetic, the obscene, the absurd, Koch tenderly guides the reader through a phantasmagoric landscape in *The Wingspan of Severed Hands*. I must confess, it's a novella I think about very often as Koch's writing continues to inspire me. Haunts me, too.

Now, onto the matter at hand, the book you're about to consume: Koch's debut collection of dark, weird, and unsettling fiction. When I was first approached by Joe to craft an introduction for their book, I paled and sensed my heart beating a little faster. Of course, I was enraptured with the idea of contributing something to their well-deserved success, but I felt such a sense of inadequacy when commissioned to speak of their skillset as an author. I still feel inadequate as I write this right now. Koch's writing is unlike anything I've ever read and, if you're new to their fiction, you'll soon discover what I mean, dear reader. Not only are their titles exceptional ("How to Fillet Angels," "The Anatomical Christ"), but their confident and exquisite command of language is catnip for admirers of poetry. Words, like the elasticity of human bodies in Koch's stories, are molded, transmuted, and rendered anew. I ask you to bear with me, dear reader, as I try to introduce you to the tales collected in this book.

When tasked with crafting a proficient prologue for this collection, I found myself struggling to capture the beauty of their writing, the visceral and haunting quality of their incomparable prose. I thought of each of the stories and contemplated whether I should analyze and prepare you for the horrors you are about to sample. But then I realized that would be such a disservice to Koch's writing seeing as their strongest asset is the element of surprise. A Joe Koch story is unlike any other story you've experienced and, therefore, should be savored like a fine wine.

I considered how to best introduce you to each of the tales Koch has expertly programmed in this inventory of debauchery. Despite my uncertainty, I found myself continually thinking of the title of the collection—*Convulsive*. A word that means "producing or consisting of convulsions." The word—convulsion—is so profoundly visceral in and of itself and taxes the mind with something almost primeval, something instinctual in our very gut. The word "convulsive" is frenetic, it's barbaric, it's supremely unnerving—all qualities I would identify as featuring significantly in Koch's writing. These stories are poignant, masterful. meaningful, bizarre, and deeply metamorphic.

Dear reader, as you near the end of this introduction and find yourself impatient to turn the page—to begin the dance, to commence the parade of obscenities—I encourage you to savor each story as I did when I first read them. I embolden you to surrender yourself to Koch's dark literary world—a nightmarish dreamscape where the human body is a paltry commodity and intended only to serve as the genesis of something new, something truly monstrous.

Perhaps at the end of your journey, you will find yourself transformed, reborn anew and thrashing in a cradle of dark viscera.

Eric LaRocca
Boston, MA
October 2021

Table of Contents

Good Paper / 10

Offerings / 16

Blood Calumny / 34

Aristotle's Lantern / 42

Rust Belt Requiescat / 54

The Anatomical Christ / 72

How To Fillet Angels / 84

The Buried King / 98

Peaveman's Lament / 104

Swanmord / 114

Mr. Bones Puzzle Candy / 130

The Revenge of Madeline Usher / 134

Mirror Grimoire / 146

The Object of Your Desire Comes Closer / 156

Paradisum Voluptatis / 170

Good Paper

Unencumbered by obscene wealth, Warynne carved out a sunspot in a city that screamed with artificial light. Under the incorrect blink of wrong colors crowding an alley, in the three a.m. silence that outlasted loud pairings, on the snow-crushed trash of a spring-thawed slope abreast a highway intersection, Warynne grew a thick, long taproot into the willing flesh of the earth. In sun, in bliss, in silence, they were alone.

Then the hawkers came.

Warynne held as still as a tree trunk, with hair like leaves that rustled in tangled gusts. No eye contact. Warynne knew better. Hawkers fed on that. One glance and they strewed their glossy pamphlets the way fish fertilize their eggs.

"Jesus loves you," they said. "Have you accepted him into your heart as your personal lord and savior?"

Warynne held fast in the taproot, in the place of expulsion. Warynne knew names like Jesus, Sampson, and David, knew faces like familiar siblings from the picture book at the top of the stairs. Cramped under the attic, behind stair rails like jail bars, behind siblings like hawkers, Warynne held fast in the taproot when Sampson was betrayed.

Two pillars flanked him. Caught in the act of crumbling, toppled from the force of the hero's hands, the temple cracked. Sampson pushed the pillars apart in disgrace, his crowning glory shorn. Curls cut away by his lover snaked across the splitting floor.

Sampson's eyes rolled back in his head, undulating globes of pain gone white. His flesh, as rendered by the artist, appeared both frail and muscular at once. Modeled pink and grey skin stretched across his strained bulk in contrast with the sharp stone of the temple. Stripped, Sampson's loincloth lilted with a taunt. Hip bones promised terror and elegance in the folds of the sparse garment.

Strong and weak, Sampson brought the temple down.

Warynne sat cross-legged at the top of the stairs with the book touching knees, hands, thighs: trembling. Mother said the bible was holy. Hers dwelled in her bedroom, tattered by triangles marking corners and leeching a smell from its leather binding like animal musk. Transparent tissue pages crackled like the potato chip bags hidden under her blankets.

Sampson in Warynne's lap was heavy and worth holding. Fearful at the touch of something holy, too young to read, Warynne caressed the multilayered lithographs on textured stock. Warynne sensed the story in Sampson's struggle between the pillars, in lolling eyes and parted lips, a navel like a gouged eye healed over, a dent in the flesh the size of a fingertip. The drape below Sampson's navel pointed at the mystery in loincloth. Under the book, another mystery Warynne was wary to touch. Linen binding left the pattern of a fine weave on Warynne's knees.

Good paper, heavy cardstock, acid-free rag, clean and un-foxed is what Warynne wants. A book worth holding, more weight than words. The picture bible is lost, stolen from some squat house or park bench. Warynne, unwilling, surrendered sanctity for survival. Forced to read, Warynne learned from mother's bible, reading and touching tissue pages while mother snuck potato chips from underneath her blankets. Warynne's words were a biblical script, imposed. Mother's bible rubbed its wrinkled leather on Warynne's hands like an old skin, a dry, ragged, hungry skin. *Read to me, Warynne*, and Warynne did, until one day reading and touching leeched the last living word from Warynne's tongue. Warynne stopped.

Mother came at Warynne from under the blankets. Potato chips and pillows blasted out. Warynne hurled the skin-covered, tissue-ridden bible at her bulk.

At the top of the stairs, under the attic, Warynne raised the heavy picture bible high. Inside, Sampson whimpered, the bad commercial rendering grown small. Mother came after his magic, came after Warynne, demanding and needing, a talking mouth intent on owning.

Suede skin like soft leather wrinkled around the mouth, pleading. Sampson's body hid the terror of the gesticulating mob behind him. Hair like snakes, snakes like cracks, cracks like fissures in the temple, shorn. Warynne ran out, mother's head uncracked, her final call a hysterical warning: *The lord has sealed my name inside your heart! You'll be back!*

Wanting, expecting, Warynne felt mother's weight until her death and sometimes after. Mother was gone, Sampson was gone, and the unbloodied picture bible burdened Warynne's backpack through seasons of snow and sweat. Warynne wanted the burden, wanted the weight.

The book is gone, stolen from some squat house or park bench. Sampson dwells in Warynne, in the taproot, in the intersection of snow-crushed ground abreast the highway, in the obscene angle of a slope faster than the slashing traffic. So fast there's not a witness. The hawkers are unhawked.

Sampson roars in grief and pushes the pillars with bony, broad-veined hands. Shorn hair wags like cracks in the pavement. Mobs spatter and unweave their integrity in the hum of traffic. Cheap glossy pamphlets flutter across eight lanes like failed fledglings. Sampson leaves the page with an agonized cry. Freed from battle, the pillars, the horns, the highway stops.

When it's dark, Warynne walks in the sun. When mother lies, Warynne's warmed. A head like Sampson's is shorn free in the crash.

The book rolls into Warynne's arms, still warm and blinking. Legs crossed, solid reliable paper stock rubbing thighs, Warynne holds the image as the eyes turn white. Imposter, cradled in Warynne's lap, palms, ecstatic fingertips, lights in hues of blue and red flash from the abscess of the highway underpass. All traffic has stopped. Warynne holds the imposter and enters the illustration. Sampson's stare is interrupted by a lascivious crevice of glue and thread that puckers between pages. Sirens rise as glue seeps from the torn skin in the blank page. Warynne smells the clean smell of good paper, the wet smell of fresh binding. Between forefinger and thumb, between siren and silence, Warynne's finger snakes through the soft wound in the skin and turns the page.

Offerings

Blaine's head hurts at the sight of Amelia shuffling up the block. Hot from raking leaves, Blaine stretches as she admires her new house in her new neighborhood. The cold pinch of October air and brisk setting sun anticipate kids pouring in tomorrow at dusk. This is prime candy territory, nothing like the streets where Blaine grew up. Children don't trick or treat in Blaine's old neighborhood, not with the fires and gunshots. Down there, they call it Devil's Night. Blaine's worked her way up and out, from dishwasher to sous chef to culinary manager. She's hosting her nieces and nephews at the new house tomorrow, and she expects to show them the flawless picture of safety and charm she's paying for. Being a member of this community doesn't come cheap. Looking down the block, it's a perfect Norman Rockwell until Amelia enters the frame.

Amelia is the neighborhood chimera. Big moist eyes, throbbing temple bones and a perpetual brood in tow mark her as an anomaly. Maybe she runs some sort of daycare. Low cost, out of her home. The couple across from Blaine points her out as *Amelia Something—do you think she even has a license?* They raise their eyebrows in knowing distaste. Fiftyish and dressed for golf no matter the day of the week, they interrogate Blaine. By the time they spot Amelia, Blaine's relieved to shift the critique to the other woman's childcare credentials. She feels wrong about it later when Amelia shambles by. Nervous and harried, Amelia wanders the upscale streets like a restless spirit locked in a magic circle of misbehaving mongrel children.

Blaine watches Amelia push the cumbersome double stroller with its side-by-side compartments for twins. It's an old design, less streamlined than the front-to-back models used by jogging moms. Amelia's posture recalls street people pushing shopping carts full of god knows what in Blaine's old neighborhood. When Blaine was a child, she shunned the faceless figures covered in rags. She'd cross the street when she saw one coming. Moving away isn't only about leaving behind the fear and filth. It's about finding a place where it's safe to be a better person, the kind of person Blaine wants to be.

Blaine hushes the hint of a headache and waves to Amelia, "Hi!"

Amelia's profile passes unaware. Her eyes face front. Sundry children scamper behind. Tomorrow morning is curbside pick-up. The children grab loose garbage from waste bins and pull recycling out of neatly bundled stacks. They drag and kick their finds down the sidewalk, inventing games as they go. After exhausting the entertainment value of an empty bottle of bleach or a discarded pizza box, they fling it onto the nearest lawn.

Amelia plods onward as cans and cartons and odd bits of trash spread through the street in her wake. She's like a tanker spewing oil.

"Hello there," Blaine calls out.

The rotten brood swarms around Amelia like flies. Although there are only three, they create the chaos of a full-blown horde. The children stop and look at Blaine, then glance at each other and continue their moving massacre.

Blaine heads down the sidewalk after them. The three children, all girls, peek back at her with feral eyes. Amelia nears the end of the block. Before she disappears around the corner, Blaine jogs to catch up and shouts, "Hello there!"

Amelia startles and turns. Her eyes are wide and glassy, her hands clutch the stroller, and her sunken face suggests nights of wakeful trance in lieu of sleep. Amelia bares her teeth and says, "Hi. How are you?"

Moments ago half the neighborhood toiled outside under autumn's vaulted light. Now it's getting dark. The birds don't chirp. Houses are barren and hushed behind festive haunted facades. Blaine does her best to return what must be Amelia's smile and says, "Good. How are you today?"

Amelia's brow furrows. Her watery blue eyes darken. She says, "Fine," without conviction or irony. The horde has spread, triangulating the two women in their sites. One girl tears apart layers of cardboard from a warped packing sheet by peeling off thin strips and waving them in the air to be taken up by the breeze. The other girls fan the air with smaller sheets of cardboard, too far away to have any effect that isn't imaginary. To Blaine's surprise, a long cardboard curl bounces on the wind, rises aloft, and then snags in the high, bare branches of a deciduous shrub.

Blaine nods at the tangle and says, "Someone's going to need a ladder to get that down."

Amelia looks baffled.

Blaine speaks up in case Amelia is hard of hearing. "They've been scattering things all over the street behind your back. I don't mean to be rude." Blaine maintains a deferential smile as Amelia stares at her wildly. Blaine gestures at the nearest shred of cardboard and then points to one of the girls. "I'm sure you want to talk to them about littering."

"Oh!" Amelia says. Her eyes bug out and zig zag around the perimeter of the triangle. Her voice is harsh. She punches out her words: "Don't do that! You're bad! Clean it up!"

The girls don't react.

Blaine stutters. "Oh no, I didn't mean—I'm so sorry, I didn't mean you should—"

On an impulse to evoke warmth, Blaine leans down to look in the stroller. Amelia blocks her. She swerves the stroller away and starts firing out questions: "Do you have a job?"

"Yes," Blaine says. "Of course."

"Where do you work?"

"A hotel."

"Which one?"

"The Kentwood Astoria."

"What do you do?"

Blaine has the urge to lie to and cross the street, feeling confronted with a shopping cart person. Instead, Blaine acts like an adult and tells part of the truth. "I work in the kitchen."

Amelia's eyes have the dark, desperate plea of a cornered animal. Her fingers twist on the stroller handle as though they can't break free. Blaine wonders if the stroller is empty. There's no movement or cooing under the blankets, no crying or kicks, and come to think of it, she's never noticed Amelia tending to any passengers in the double compartments.

Amelia smiles again, but she looks more like she's in pain. She says, "I wish I had a job like that."

"It's great. I love to cook. Always have." Blaine doesn't tell Amelia she's the culinary manager of both restaurants in the hotel. She doesn't offer Amelia a job. "Planning, making everything just right. You know what I mean." Amelia stares. The girls amble in closer. Blaine chatters. "You'd think after fifty, sixty hours a week I wouldn't want to do the same thing at home, but I love it. In fact, you know, I really have to go. My nieces and nephews are coming over to trick or treat tomorrow." The girls saunter up behind Amelia like cowboys challenging Blaine to a draw. Blaine clears her throat to cover up an inappropriate laugh at the absurd image. In the silent intensity of their stares, Blaine says, "Why don't you drop by?"

Amelia says, "Oh. Okay."

The girls remain inscrutable.

"I'm sorry," Blaine says. "I have to go. I didn't mean to be rude earlier. I can't imagine. It must be hard for you, with so many."

Amelia's eyes seek the horizon like a shipwreck victim. She looks over Blaine's shoulder and speaks to the vanishing point in the distance. She says, "They're not mine."

‡

Blaine can't lie to herself. She's relieved when Amelia doesn't show up.

The house has been silent for at least an hour when the doorbell rings. The house is too quiet with the party over and the kids all gone, or maybe for Blaine, it's just quiet enough. Blaine's not sure she'll ever be ready to have children, not after what she saw in Amelia's eyes last night. She's been savoring the adult version of the witch's brew punch and contemplating her goals when the doorbell interrupts. It's ten-thirty.

Through a sliver in the curtains, Blaine spies Amelia clutching the stroller handle. She's at the end of the walkway near the street, almost out of range of the porch light. In the dark, the stroller looks more like a shopping cart mounded with hoardings of homeless life than it does in the daytime. Amelia's eyes jump from Blaine's front steps to flutter moth-like at the motion in the window. Her mouth stretches into a desperate leer. Blaine sighs. A headache threatens. Placing her cocktail on the mantel, Blaine grabs a handful of good chocolate. The kiddie stuff is all gone. She wonders why the hell Amelia has the children out so late.

The three girls present pillowcases faded and tattered from too many wash cycles. Frayed edges sag in tiny, expectant hands. The children wear the same clothes they had on yesterday when they plundered the garbage. Their only costumes are their masks. Blaine forces herself to say, "Well, aren't you cute," as she drops chocolate into each threadbare sack.

The masks look realistic, like expensive theater props. Blaine appreciates the quality, but not the content. The first girl wears an Inuit-style bird head with spiraling hypnotic eyes and blood oozing from its beak. As the blood accumulates, it drips on the girl's clothes. The head is plumed with what appear to be authentic feathers that rustle when she receives her candy. The second girl has the red face of a devil with hairy ears, gnarled fangs and a long forked tongue that lolls out of the side of her mouth. In place of a nose, the devil face sports a fully formed miniature devil with arms, legs and tail that dances and gestures. The tiny devil double mutters and drives at the air with a pitchfork. The third girl is a faceless, pink, flabby thing with several soft, rounded horns that protrude from the top of her head. The horns are more like knobby tentacles or snakes that stretch and enlarge at the ends. They bob and pulsate with engorged veins along the shaft like a vulgar pseudo-medical device. When Blaine gives her candy, the horns throb and lilt.

Amelia grins.

Blaine does her best to keep smiling at the masks. She's given away all the chocolate and the girls don't move to go. Neither does Amelia. Blaine turns her palms outward and then clasps them together. "Well," she says, "Trick or treat."

Amelia yells, "Say it!"

"Wik yur ree," the girls mumble under their masks. Then the smallest girl, the one with the flabby tentacles on her head says, "I gotta go potty."

Amelia doesn't respond. Her teeth are clenched like a fiend and her watery blue eyes are frozen into hard, round marbles. The little girl bends her knees and bounces, pressing her hands between her legs. Her flabby horns wobble. "I gotta go now!"

"Okay, hon. Come on." Blaine grabs the little girl's hand and takes her to the guest bathroom. The protrusions nudge Blaine's forearm. Blaine isn't sure if she's more disgusted by the physical sensation of the soft horns or by the behavior of the girl's mother. Or whatever Amelia is supposed to be. Blaine kneels, eye-level with the eyeless face. She asks, "Do you need any help?" The little girl giggles and slams the bathroom door.

Blaine wonders how the child can see anything from inside the mask. She hopes she can take it off on her own. After several minutes of quiet, Blaine says, "How are you doing?" There's no answer. Blaine tries the door handle. It's locked. Blaine taps a few times. "Is everything okay?" The toilet flushes and the girl bursts through into Blaine's arms. Blaine catches her and asks, "Did you forget to wash your hands?" The girl shakes her head, jiggling the mask's rubbery horns. She squirms out of Blaine's grasp and runs away.

Cold air and scraps of leaf litter from the street tumble into Blaine's living room through the open front door. The girls sprawl on Blaine's Persian rug sorting mountains of candy. Their tattered pillowcases drape the room. A statue of Kuan Yin sticks her sutra out from under a worn floral pattern. Soil and rocks spill from a houseplant trampled by a herd of threadbare unicorns. Pink polka dots clash with tasteful earth tone upholstery. Blaine rushes past the disaster to fetch Amelia from outside.

The walkway is empty. The street is deserted. Blaine looks up and down the block and jogs to the corner, passing plastic gravestones and cardboard skeletons. She runs to the opposite corner, searching by the orange glow of jack-o-lanterns with wicked smiles that share an inside joke. Heading back up the other side, black cat decals mock Blaine's panic with cartoon anxiety in their eyes. Swaying effigies of an old green-faced witch nod wisely, warning Blaine to be mindful of the historical fate of unconventional women. The same black-cloaked dolls with pointed caps hang from every porch except for Blaine's, as though marking her lack of affinity with some unspoken tradition. Amelia is nowhere in sight.

"Damn her," Blaine whispers.

Returning to the brood, Blaine crouches on the living room carpet. All three girls wear their masks. They sort candy in silence. Starting with the largest piece, regardless of flavor, color or type, they arrange stacks to achieve an even distribution of mass. Little hands weigh and move the candy each time the job appears done. Blaine guesses it must be a game with rules only the girls understand.

The dissimilarity of the girls with other children leaves Blaine unsure how to act. Earlier, when her brother's youngest spilled red pop on her pants, Blaine improvised a new costume bottom with a pair of patterned leggings. The girl stopped crying, the others quit teasing, and all of the children got curious about the hidden treasures in Aunt Blaine's closet. Blaine raided her wardrobe for accessories and ended up hosting a side party in her bedroom and dressing up with the kids. Her siblings looked at her askance, but it was more fun than listening to her brother-in-law pontificate about current events.

Blaine breaks the silence. "That's quite a haul. Looks like you guys hit the jackpot tonight."

The girls continue their candy game with the gravity of old men playing poker. They don't eat any candy. They don't battle or bargain for favorites. They measure and sort.

"Which one do you like best?" Blaine asks.

None of the girls says a word.

Blaine takes a small cellophane bag of candy corn out of the middle pile and tears it open with her teeth. "You don't mind if I have this one, right?"

She's got the girls' attention. They stop playing and turn toward Blaine while she chews the sugary tidbits. The candy is so sweet it's almost painful to eat. Blaine says, "Did Miss Amelia tell you where she was going?"

Facing Blaine, the girls don't answer or resume their game. They sit still except for the unnatural movement of the masks.

"Can you tell me where Miss Amelia went, or make a guess for me? Did she say anything before she left?"

The bird mask rolls its spiraling eyes in exasperation. The devil nose smirks. The flaccid horns quiver.

"Has she done this before? Where does she go?"

The autonomous devil nose can't contain itself any longer. It blurts, "She can go to Hell!"

Blaine keeps chewing as the nose does a little dance and the face around it glows a deeper shade of red. Blaine's amazed by the craftsmanship. She can't see any wires or strings. She says, "You look like you'd know the way there."

All three girls burst out laughing.

Blaine isn't sure if laughter is progress, but it's better than weird silence. She addresses the autonomous devil nose. "Excuse me, sir. We haven't been properly introduced. My name is Blaine. What's your name?"

The miniature devil raises its pitchfork. The girls chant in happy unison like a squad of cheerleaders: "We are Legion!"

"I see," Blaine says. "So you're little demons tonight."

The masks nod with enthusiasm.

Blaine rises and gathers the discarded pillowcases from around the room. "Being supernatural and all, I know you're not tired, but it's getting pretty late." She picks up candy and drops it into the bags. "I'm sure all of you know that if demons don't get back to Hell before midnight they turn back into regular boring girls."

The masks confer quickly. Blood-beak points her hypnotic spiraling eyes at Blaine. "That's not true! You're lying."

Blaine shrugs off the accusing stare. The eyes make her dizzy if she looks for too long. "Find out for yourself then." She shovels candy off the floor with both hands and fills up the sacks. The girls try to stop her and pull the candy back out. Blaine is bigger and faster and competitive by nature. She pins a full pillowcase closed with her knee and uses her elbows to block the girls' assault. Hands slap and bump and grab. Wrappers tear and candy colors smudge under fingernails. Blaine's breathless as she presents each girl with a full pillowcase in triumph. "Okay. Come on, let's get up and go."

Blood-beak says, "Go where?"

"Home," Blaine says. "Lead the way."

Devil-nose is the biggest girl. She cocks her head to one side and says, "We are home, dummy."

Blood-beak concurs, "You'll get used to it."

"Nope," Blaine says. "You're evicted. Up and out."

Devil-nose lifts her pillowcase as high in the air as her arms can reach and turns it upside down. Candy bounces across the carpet, rolls under the chairs and coffee table, and lodges between the end tables and couch. Detached wrappers drift and scatter into every corner. The other girls follow her lead and do the same. Then they count to three and toss their empty pillowcases into the air and clap. The sacks parachute over the room like jovial ghosts at play.

"Fine," Blaine says, taking the smallest girl's arm, the shy one with the wobbly horns on her faceless head. "You can go without your candy."

Horn-head's body goes slack. Her arm is dead weight in Blaine's grip. She wails, "No, Mommy, no. I don't like this game." Blaine tries to hold her so she'll stand up, but the child collapses in tears and rolls as if she's in agony, crushing warm candy into the rug.

Devil-nose rushes to comfort little Horn-head, clutching her tight and rolling along with her. "Look what you did. You made her cry!"

Blood-beak flings her feathers at Blaine before she joins. "You're supposed to be nice!"

Something slick splatters Blaine's face. The girls wrestle in a confusion of animal parts and totem heads. The smallest one cries: "Mommy, mommy, don't make me leave you!" The others scream the same words in repeated torment and mocking laughter. The miniature devil on the biggest girl's nose brays and squeals. Blaine feels dizzy and insane, like she's watching a pen of cannibal pigs mangle each other on her living room floor.

The cacophony of laughter and piercing wails from the girls stabs Blaine's temples. She says, "Stop it" uselessly. The roiling mass expands and engulfs her like a migraine. Her head pounds until she realizes that the pounding is outside her skull, on her front door, where a fist demands an answer. Blaine lunges and almost falls into a blinding light. It's the police.

Two officers stand on the threshold. One shines a flashlight inside and says, "Excuse me, ma'am. Is everything alright here?"

"Oh no, no it's not," Blaine says. "Please, come in."

The officers exchange a look and step inside. Behind them, the deserted street has come to life, not with roaming ghosts but with peering neighbors, open storm doors and illuminated porch lights. The black witch effigy dolls are lit from behind, casting shadows. They sway on their brooms, titillating lurid whispers up and down the block.

The girls cling to Blaine's legs like baby marsupials cowering from a threat. Blaine gestures at the creatures with open palms. "Their mother left them here. Or babysitter. This is so terrible, the poor things. Please, can you get them home?"

"What's the address, ma'am?"

"I don't know."

"Have you called their mother?"

"I don't have a number. Her name's Amelia."

"Amelia what?"

"I don't know. Everyone knows her. Ask one of those people." Blaine points over the crush of the girls at the peeping faces outside. The officer with the flashlight lowers it, and then turns and shuts the front door. The last thing Blaine sees outside is the neighbor couple in matching bathrobes pulling their witch doll down from the rafters.

The second officer buddies up next to Blaine and the girls while Flashlight scans the scene. The girls press into Blaine. Devil teeth snag holes in Blaine's sweatpants. Blood drips from the beak and dampens her thighs. Flabby horns writhe on her like hungry worms.

Blaine pushes back at the girls. Her fingers sink into the horns like chewed bubblegum. The bloody beak nips at her wrist. "Jesus," she says, "Get them off me."

Flashlight says, "Calm down, ma'am."

Buddy admonishes, "You shouldn't talk that way in front of the children."

Blaine knows she's got blood from the bird-beak spattered across her forehead and her ponytail has fallen halfway out. Smeared candy sticks to the carpet, Kuan Yin lies prone among used pillowcases and shredded wrappers, and watery dirt from the house plant spreads a black stain on the hardwood floor. Blaine tries to act more reasonable than she appears. "Please," she says, "Can you take them? Their mother must be worried sick."

From the mantle, there's a loud *chink* as the ice melts in Blaine's cocktail glass.

Flashlight says, "Have you been drinking?"

"I made punch," Blaine says. "For my family."

"Is that a yes, ma'am?"

Blaine says, "It's not like that. It was mostly children."

"Where's your husband?"

"I'm single."

"Three kids and not married," Flashlight says to Buddy.

Blaine starts to protest and Buddy comes to her defense. "Things are different now than when we were coming up. You can't judge girls these days, what with women's lib and them having to work and all. Be glad it's not the drugs."

Flashlight shakes his head at Blaine. "I guess I'm just old-fashioned."

Blaine struggles against the girls. "Look, you don't get it.

Listen—ouch, stop it!"

Flashlight kneels next to Blaine and speaks to Blood-beak. "Hi, sweetheart. You look really scary tonight. Did your mommy help you with your costume?"

Blood-beak says proudly, "No. I made it all by myself."

"How about that?" says Flashlight. "What's all over your mouth?"

"Candy."

"Is that what you call it? It looks pretty messy. Did you eat too much candy tonight?"

"No, sir."

"What about mommy? Did mommy have too much fun and get messy?"

Blood-beak says, "She invited us, sir."

Blaine says, "What does this have to do with—get them off me!"

Flashlight says, "Do you think you can be good for mommy tonight?"

"For Christ's sake," Blaine says. "I'm not—"

Flashlight cuts her off sternly. "How much have you had to drink tonight, ma'am?"

"Two glasses of punch. Who cares?"

Buddy explains: "See, honey, if you blow point-oh-eight it's a mandatory report. We have an obligation."

"Report what? This is my house."

"We have to call protective services. It's mandatory."

"Are you crazy?"

Flashlight stands and puts his hand near his holster. "Just relax, ma'am. There's no need for talk like that. Answer the question. Are you the sole caretaker of these children? Is there anyone else here?"

"No, but—"

"Seems like she lives alone, then," Flashlight says to Buddy.

Buddy shrugs. "Yeah. Too bad she didn't drink much. It's gonna be rough."

Flashlight checks the scene once more and moves toward the door. He declares: "The only substance I see being abused here is sugar."

Buddy says, "You got that right."

"Wait," Blaine says. "What about them?"

"Mommy, you're so funny." The girls laugh and hug Blaine's legs like a Chinese finger trap. The more she struggles, the tighter they grip.

Buddy tells Blaine, "I'd try to relax more if I were you."

The girls join their small hands and close the ring tighter around Blaine. They spin Blaine against her will as they circle and begin to sing a nursery rhyme. Blaine cries out, "Wait. Report me. Take them away. Please."

Buddy's eyes follow the counter-clockwise motion of the girls spinning Blaine around and around. He frowns at Flashlight. "I hope she can handle them better than the last one. What do we tell the Connors about Riley?"

Blaine shouts: "Hey. Arrest me. Get me out of here."

Flashlight says, "I don't think we need to make a big deal out of a few extra treats on Halloween. Everyone knows the risks."

"True," Buddy says. He turns to Blaine once more. "We'll let it slide this one time. We know it's hard being a single mom, especially when you have so many."

Blaine's voice succumbs to the sing-song chant of the girls as Buddy and Flashlight lock the door behind them. Blaine mouths the muted words: *They're not mine.*

The chant pulsates around her. The song is a nursery rhyme Blaine doesn't recognize in a language she can't understand. Her head throbs in cadence with the repetitive melody as she spins. The girls distort and expand, forming a membranous skin. Blaine punches at the elastic mass enclosing her. It absorbs her effort and warps back into place. She tries to aim for their faces and fails. It's impossible for Blaine to single out the individual masks in the spinning swarm of devil laugh, razor beak and warm flesh. Blaine can see everything clearly, but her mind can't process what she sees. The girls have sloughed off their street clothes. Their bodies are the same as their faces. Their faces are not masks.

‡

At the edge of an empty ballpark, a baby stroller waits outside in the dark. It's a cumbersome double stroller, the type with side-by-side seating compartments for twins. An autumn frost coats the bulky shape, highlighting it under the glow of the Hunter's moon against a backdrop of pines.

If a curious passerby stops, they breathe easy to notice no sound or motion from the abandoned stroller. Coming near, they worry about what they'll find tucked underneath the blanket. The worn coverlet appears to be decorated with alphabet blocks, but upon closer inspection, the symbols look more like ancient runes. Thinking twice about using their bare hands, the curious observer searches the ground for a fallen branch. They lift the weather-stained blanket, revealing a vacuum of darkness inside the stroller compartments blacker than the surrounding night. A flash of deeper, greater darkness from within startles them. They drop the branch, and it's sucked away. There's a crackling sound, as if something unseen is trying to eat the branch.

Another crackling sound resonates across the park. At the crest of a hill, the neighborhood is gathered around a bonfire. It's the end of October again, the transitional time between fall and winter. Until the New Year begins on the morning after Halloween, the fate of the community hangs in the balance. The veil is thin, and everything can change tonight. With equal reverence and revelry, the neighborhood residents wait for the cutty black sow to show her face and give herself up as an offering.

Blaine doesn't hear the bonfire or the crackling of the branch from the double stroller compartments. She hears the hungry crying of its passenger. Blaine experiences the crying as a direct bond, as her own insatiable need. The rest of the world is barely audible. As Blaine practices leaving the stroller unattended for longer and more agonizing stretches of time, the sound of crying never stops. When Blaine grasps the handle once again, she's flooded with a sickening relief. Then she's compelled to push. The giggling girls encircle her, swarming and weaving in a chaotic orbit. One full year of Blaine's life has passed this way.

Near the bonfire, Blaine's neighbors watch with orange

faces, lit by flame. The couple in golf clothes gropes one another with weird delight. Flashlight and Buddy stand at attention, solemn in their fire safety gear. Other familiar faces leer, faces Blaine can't associate with names, joggers and gardeners and pedigreed dog walkers. All grow hideous with grotesque laughter, spitting and popping like logs in the fire, grinning like jack-o-lanterns sharing an inside joke.

Blaine's exhausted from a year of service, a year of keeping the girls well-fed with scraps and travelers from the hotel, a year of constant need and no rest. Blaine sees an easy answer in the beckoning flames.

Lucky for her, the girls are good at keeping secrets. Blaine's primed them as much as she can. They're excited she wants to play dress up and they've been rehearsing every day. Tonight is their big chance. The girls leap as the stroller hits the bonfire. Blood-beak jabs her maw deep between Blaine's thoracic vertebrae and into her spinal column. After a rupture of pain, powerful wings emerge from Blaine's back. Blaine feels stronger and lighter. She begs her hands to release the stroller. Gravity helps them comply. As Blaine rises, Devil-nose plunges down her throat. Blaine feels like she's choking until a long, fiery tongue snakes its way over her esophagus and out of her mouth. She sprays fire on the crowd below. The last girl, faceless and soft-horned, clings whining around Blaine's waist. She's the youngest of the three and needs a little push. Blaine coaxes her gently and reminds her of the plan. They merge, and a glorious Leviathan unfolds beneath Blaine's wings.

The stroller rolls down the hill, unmothered and ablaze. The crowd chases it in frenzy. Blaine lays them to waste. No one remains to save the stroller from burning. No one is left to hold the maw of the portal open and allow the unseen occupant to gape into a world where it doesn't belong. The passenger is banished. The crying abates. The October sky glows amber and red, and the mythical beast Blaine has become circles the neighborhood and pumps its majestic wings. It rises higher and higher in an ascending orbit above the trees and wraps itself in wisps of cloud. It folds its wings and settles into the sky. Drifting across the moon's silhouette in a chimera-shaped nest, the beast slips into an unspoiled sleep.

[redacted]

Blood Calumny

Kevin didn't want to share a room with their mother. In the tiny house after the divorce, she said they didn't have a choice. Telling this to Bastien while lighting a cigarette to appear casual, because their hands and mouth need something to do in the huge chasm between speaking and waiting to be judged, need anything other than Bastien's hurt silence, Bastien's head turning away; Kevin insists it's nothing personal. "It's not you, it's me. I can't be with anyone. Not like this."

Alone again, because it's what they asked for—now isn't it? Kevin crushes what's left of their cigarette, dumps the contents of the ashtray in the outdoor bin, and washes their hands longer than they really need to. Puts the ashtray in the nightstand drawer with the remnants of a pack of camels, a bad brand and a bad habit from college that Kevin gave up years ago.

Well, mostly gave up. Kevin's not a saint.

They're not responsible for what it does though, either, because it's not their choice, it never has been, and if Bastien or anyone else could understand—but they can't. The blood, the tears, the murders—and now that Kevin's older, the heat, the rage, the unpredictable eruptions that never came like clockwork and come now hard with increasing frequency and capricious vengeance against the host. The parasite people call a blessing.

It's not like Kevin hasn't tried to have it taken out.

Planned Parenthood in nineteen eighty-seven, University

Women's Center in nineteen ninety-two, Ladies First Fem-Care in ninety-nine, Planned Parenthood again in zero-one, Sweet Valley Whole Woman's Health in twenty-ten, and on and on for nearly fifty years, a litany of providers saying *dear* and *hon* and *Miss Kevin,* reciting a litany of excuses with clucking tongues. It doesn't matter if Kevin's a big, hairy guy waving money in their faces and begging them to get the monster out. The minute Kevin hits an exam table, the clucking starts.

Left to take matters into their own hands, Kevin closes the tobacco drawer in the nightstand. Modelled on an apothecary cabinet with eight stacked compartments, it hides a hatch holding errata shipped across the country after their father died. Masculine objects recall life before the onset: coins, pocket knives, a rusted harmonica, marbles, an old watch. Kevin decides on a military folding knife with a three-and-a-half-inch blade. Opens the knife and places it next to their phone charger in easy reach.

In the tiny house, after the divorce, sharing a room with mom because the girls were older, the girls deserved privacy, Kevin's arguments dismissed as selfish. Kevin can't sleep. Not with their mother fighting off blankets like an invisible assailant. The house asleep, the world asleep, their mother unconscious, Kevin cornered in the extra bed between the thrashing woman and the bedroom door. Her sleeping body kicks and flails. Face flops over in Kevin's direction, pouring sweat. A smile crawls onto her slack lips. Mouth emits a pleasured moan. There's a smell of rotten musk; something meaty and slippery releases itself from tangled legs and sheets. Wet noises slop out, and a limping shadow skulks away, wandering the walls and ceiling in the darkness. Kevin freezes, stares, tracks its progress. Lumbering like a giant slug, thick and moist, it blends into the rustling curtains and merges with tossed blankets. It unfurls in recessed corners where the moonlight can't reach. Dangles for an hour above Kevin's toy chest; sways like an extra appendage from the ceiling lamp. Swims through pools of shadow poured between furniture and floor. Finally prowling to the foot of their mother's bed, turning in circles like an angry cat, it wiggles beneath the disordered covers and squeezes back into its hiding place with a loud pop.

In the morning, Kevin's mother tries to hide the stain. *Don't be scared. I'm going through the change. Someday you'll understand.*

Sometimes in the suppurating nighttime shadows, it gets lost. Meandering senile, perched atop a tall dresser next to their mother's handbag, working its two thick, prehensile loops around to imitate the shape. Thudding on the floor and lying immobile for hours as if drunk. Kevin can't hide in the bathroom or stay awake all night watching the wandering lump of shiny musculature with its trailing webs of fat. Sooner or later, Kevin has to sleep.

One night they wake up in the dark. Their mother snores. Stuffed animals guard the L-shaped perimeter of Kevin's cramped bed. Kevin reaches for the safety of a favorite plush elephant, its floppy ears deformed by moonlight. The soft, furry body presses against Kevin's chest, but the trunk is slick, wet, and smelly. Kevin doesn't remember dropping the toy in the toilet or having an accident.

When they understand what their senses are saying, it's too late to throw the thing against the wall and escape its embrace.

If Kevin tried to explain the invasion to Bastien, imagine the derision. *You're not telling me you really believe that, are you? All kids have bad dreams.* Yes, Kevin would have to confirm. That is exactly what they believe. And then Kevin would have to talk about the murders.

Because it's never been enough for the parasite to co-opt a habitat inside Kevin's body, first snip, snip, snipping away at the natural epithelial barrier, then ballooning inward with murderous suction, and last looping its flexible appended egg sacs through painful ligatures, stringing bubble-soft proliferations within the cradle of Kevin's bones. Kevin's mother exhausted as a host, the parasite throbbing with new life. Kevin clotted with abdominal gristle as it spits irregular blood. Wandering still, it comes back sated with strange blood; black, brown, elastic, and stringy; smelling of foreign anatomies; pitted with liverish clumps. What it kills, Kevin never questions. It moves like a thief. Kevin catches it with the knife.

Marks on the nightstand, the mattress, the hardwood floor: failed impalements. Kevin feels it fighting dormancy as they age, yet still it weighs heavy, holding on inside them between erratic manic travels and explosive gore. Gone for days, maybe a whole week now, and god knows Bastien can't be allowed to stay over, can't be the next witness or victim; Kevin waits alone, armed as the sun goes down, pretending to sleep. A shadow in the dark, a lump in the sheets. All the reasons Kevin never lets a lover spend the night.

It rears. Kevin strikes.

Try explaining the knife to Bastien, the cries of the thing strong and unruly after a bloody jaunt. Insistent on its territorial claim to Kevin, it wrestles with smooth muscle and fallopian fists though stabbed and blubbering. If it squealed madly, Kevin might have the guts to kill it. Instead, pinned on the nightstand, slickly twisting, globs of empathic fat flinging, it weeps. Coagulates of mourning, choruses of outrage for the loud injustices against those who bear it, the parasite pleads for the oneness of mercy.

Did she know?

Kevin wonders, and doubt destroys resolve. Litanies of maybe, of anti-abraxas, of Hecate burning. Earthly trinities work their binding legacy upon Kevin's unquiet rebellion, begging acceptance. The subtle ache and absence. The horror cloying, wet, and warm. The spongy egg sacs sticking to Kevin's wrist, parasite climbing their arm, ripping open as it pulls free of the severing blade. Escapes the knife with its fundus spliced.

It sticks, and Kevin can't resist. Piercing like a mole, it spreads where Kevin is tender, working them apart. It lingers with maternal affinity. That in which Kevin gestated now gestates angrily inside them.

Kevin coughs up a clot of blonde hair in the kitchen sink. They know better than to risk the bathroom where the mirror reflects a true crime lineup of lost lives. A dead-naming phlebotomist. A cop minimizing a threat. Store clerks saying ma'am. Strangers telling them to smile. Vengeance perpetrated against ignorant offenders, inconsistent visions shared by the parasite in its homing state, dreaming as Kevin vomits guilt like a reluctant, unborn twin.

Worst are the unknown trolls, the faces Kevin can't

recognize, for unlike the foreign thing that hunts and comes back to nest in their body, Kevin can't read thoughts. They've cancelled all their social accounts. They plug their ears when gossip starts. Kevin can't carry the burden of the parasite's reprisals. They curse the media for broadcasting the personal opinions of the rich and famous, for encouraging discourse as if embedded bias was up for debate. Every keyword blocked, news seeps through.

Kevin agrees with the parasite that hatred is not negotiable. The sight of the beloved icon's face bloated in strangulation, hair swathed around the neck and laced over the eyes like a perverse wedding veil, her swollen tongue popping through the long, blonde gauze, its red tip turning grey; the outcry of fans in grief and shock; it's too much for Kevin to bear.

Nine-one-one to report a crime. Alone in the dark, the shadow lump listening inside, oh god, it knows, please hurry; Kevin waits for a call back. A sarcastic operator, another transferred call. After midnight, with instructions to stay home, they wait for the detective to follow up. Hours later, a ringtone Kevin hardly recognizes. A deep, weary monotone.

So your uterus wanders–

Not mine. Hers. My mother.

Okay, so your mother's uterus wanders around killing people.

Yes.

But it lives inside you.

Yes.

And it's happened before. The killing.

Well, yes.

And you didn't do anything to stop it?

You don't understand. I–

We have a witness that places you in your home on the night in question at ten. How did you cross the Atlantic so fast?

I told you, it's not me–

Oh right, right. So your little friend did it.

If you insist on calling it that.

Sorry, your mother's little friend. Did it sprout little wings?

I–I just want it to stop.

Let me give you a bit of advice. My wife is about your age and she–

Kevin fumbles and hangs up.

The creature stirs. Morning's half-light quiets its rumblings, but there's no doubt the tenor of Kevin's restless night has renewed the prospective hit list. *Half the local police force*, Kevin frets, trying their best not to wish ill on the patronizing bastards, trying not to fuel the fire with vengeful thoughts. Perhaps the parasite wants nothing more than respect, like an old person sent out to pasture. It's old, at least twice as old as Kevin, and who knows how old it was before it made its way into their mother's mind, body, life.

Did she know?

Kevin hunts for clues in her curse: *Someday you'll understand.*

In response, the restless, kindred organ stretches its misplaced muscles, releasing a fast, unexpected river of blood that shoots down Kevin's leg. Pooled in their shoe, streaked on pants and bedding, splattered on the floor all the way to the bathroom in lavish drops. A bristling sensation of needles feeds on their skin. If Kevin questions how much their mother loved them, they dismiss the obvious answer in a heated decision during clean-up.

Quick, on the phone, before they lose their nerve: "I've been thinking it over. What you said about moving forward."

Bastien, wary as hell: "What happened last night? The fucking police called."

"The thing is this. I think you're right. It's time I quit running away from commitment."

"You do? Why now?"

Kevin, biting their lip. If there were any other way—but Kevin's done their time serving the unwanted inheritance. Bastien is young enough to handle the legacy, young enough to fight off public calumny, a generation younger than Kevin and reared on social justice. Bastien doesn't have murderous thoughts like Kevin, and if they find out no one can kill it—

Kevin says, "Do you want to come over and spend the night?"

[redacted]

Aristotle's Lantern

In the opening sequence, we see the beat, the rush, the car crash. It reads as the end, but, for Adrasteia, it's the start of the shoot. In the jump-cut logic of the film, the last scene is when she shines. The curtain drops, and Adrasteia opens wide. Wide victim eyes. Where she is, she doesn't know. Dark place. Harpoon edges. Stink of fish meat. Adrasteia scrambles for a beacon, trawls inward for an unbroken line. She'll have flashbacks of how the men gathered, the sound of the ignition sputtering, the pervasive wetness. So much debris they fit inside of her. How soon after release the film stock starts to rot. In a few years, or seconds, it won't matter what they do to her body, because, in the long run, the body dies, and the soul forgets.

Aware after impact, diegetic dripping sounds in her field of vision. Hanging. The men in various corners. The nightmare knowledge that there is no way out. The giggling man, before he senses her presence. Close up on his work bench. Cut to Adrasteia's eyes. Precious prequel seconds in shadow. High contrast lights. Shaky camera. Clicking sounds. The moment to run lost. Her silent shock legitimizes a gore discourse with urban legends. When rough hands take her down, Adrasteia doesn't scream.

Frames shuffle like cards. The viewer feels disoriented, a kidnap victim when the hood comes off. Attrition subverts narrative lucidity due to incompetence or cinematic design. The result is that the viewer is forced to work harder to follow the shattered plot and is exhausted into submission. If they don't walk out in rage, they accept their passive stance and let the violence wash over them. Likewise, Adrasteia, in the role of her death-time, grinds downward from denial to grasping, from savior to grave. Her head seeks a hero, awash in nihilist disbelief. No way out. Nothing she's done to deserve this. Her fatal mistake was being born.

Pan to the giggling man. Rotted seafood texture of cinéma vérité. Car crash graphics. Homicide stock. Blurbs across Adrasteia's body, schoolgirl uniform ripped. Found footage warnings in red splatter letters. Life is cheap. Redemption is impossible. There will be no coming of age.

Jump cut to adult. Praying naked with a mouth full of razorblades, Adrasteia argues the minutiae of autonomy through restrained gestures. The set remains the same. The men haven't aged. She seeks to please her captors with a hospital mimesis counted out in five-four time. Scraping, she never weeps. Her posture, as defined by the surrounding wreckage of bodies, offends the viewer with a livelier set of fetishes.

Her involuntary desire to trust. The heart of a child. The light of silence bejeweling her tongue. A crack in the free-floating bone Adrasteia keeps latched. Backstory submerged in sequential dissonance, dark and silent as a severed head thrown into the sea.

Her silence is silver. It's X-ACTO®-knife sharp, made of ingrown blades. The tightening collet of redacted lines pinches her mouth shut. Never tell. Don't bother to scream. Don't cry for help. The call is coming from inside your mouth.

Adolescent flash forward. Adrasteia was born for this scene. All her life, she thinks, or was taught to think, or began to think—when she started getting into character because there was no other way to turn except inward and deeper—she was meant to hold calisthenic ejaculations and recycled glass in full public view without complaint.

The soon-severed head of Adrasteia isn't empty, though it floats above her body in the film's aftermath. It's too soft-spoken for the average oracular snuff film fan to enjoy her radial cephalization. Adrasteia reads her own thoughts, forgotten prophecies sourced from external kicks in the teeth and unprocessed grief.

An intrusive voice-over speaks for the mute actress.

"The men are laughing at you. You have clots in your knees. You can't wait for your head to get cut off, yet you bargain for delays like a miser and take it up the blowhole, great and white. You'll regret it if you live to tell the tale."

Her silence is ship's brass. It oxidizes with the inconsistency of genital warts. When another missile erupts, Adrasteia colors it pink with froth from her saved saliva. From sores in her mouth that still bleed. What the men have done with her so far is nothing compared to what happens in the second and third films. The sequels bleach her horns faster than Adrasteia can shave off their weight. She remains inescapable.

It's a hoax, of course. The most basic critical analysis leaves no question in the viewer's mind that Adrasteia doesn't survive.

Wide shot. One man collapses like a hangover. One is worn out, one hiding, and another prepares fresh handfuls of razorblades extracted from last year's candy. He'll use the slender devices to compromise the nemeses inside Adrasteia's body. There's a consensus among the men that she needs new teeth.

The amateur operation isn't meant to cure her ordeal or enhance longevity. It's purely for fun. By the time it's over, the internal pain of calculated edges proves every motion of her pelvis a slice.

Her role requires consent, and the call to action catches her off-kilter. With the next scene on deck, the camera is sinking, sliding. The set rests on salts, on channeled lungs, and keening waters. Speak no more of your missing daughters. Adrasteia reaches underside in agony according to the implicit script. She's retracted by habit. Jailbait Gehenna constant, with movable spines. The men laugh at the sight of her susceptible decline.

The viewer can't tell when the scene happens, or how old Adrasteia is meant to be, due to the obfuscation of blood. Other than the notorious coda, this scene is a favorite among fans. Adrasteia fingers herself and loses another digit. One man hoots, one threatens death if she stops, and another martyrs an existence fragrant with lost children, for he himself is lost. Where he spills his sperm, hopes die.

Adrasteia's thumb pops off. Her acting is strained and desperate, trying the patience of her costars. Perhaps it's the contrast between agonized facial contortions and her muteness that creates an accidental comic effect, thus alienating the viewer's sympathies. The men engage in casual debate, trying to decide if it's still fisting when all that's left of her hand is a bloody nub.

The enticement of decay is too pungent to dismiss as mere crisis. The men circle Adrasteia, rattling dice. Wreaths of cilia extend like seaweed from her ears, exaggerating every sound. She can count how long she's been here by measuring the distance the fine hairs travel towards surface or solace. Silky woven ropes bind her head in stillness, aggravated by anaphylactic sex. The old familiar voice-over is near null, near prophet.

"The getaway car crashed before you were conceived as a spark. You will not escape the last scene alive. Where invertebrates fear to tread…well, you know the rest. Cozy up to a gaffer if you want more light."

The intrusive narration further distances the viewer from the immediacy of the extended torture scene, placing them outside a dirty fish tank peering in through layers of algae. This approach wears down the viewer's strained gaze and degrades the eye by means of squalid production values and haphazard editorial choices less amateur than malicious. If art gives, this takes.

The viewer feels detached, dirty, and used. It's all her fault. Just look at that bitch groveling under the pointed indifference of the camera lens. Listen to her silence. The sound of a body in distress. The harbinger of irreparable damage to come. Adrasteia shrinks audibly from the knife-like rays strobing her throat in close-up.

Adrasteia is inevitable, like some underwater nun. Her vow of silence is chlamydial. Its side effect is time travel. Adrasteia everywhere: in the fish tank, in the viewer's lap, in the critic's eye. Her absence from her body stinks up the set. The viewer feels both disgusted and aroused by the growing odor. The giggling man winks at the fourth wall. Complicit critics spread her scent through nasal telepathy. The men and their understudies develop a taste for rare bacteria endemic to Adrasteia's injuries. The more disease they squeeze out of her, the greater their thieves' delight.

They dance raucously around the victim and sing a shanty, hooked elbows a-circling. Adrasteia is disarmed by the lack of continuity. How the hell is she supposed to detonate? Her role is already challenging enough. The self she plays in opposition to her deeper oceanic death necessitates escape by preventing its possibility. The men surround her, singing, stomping out a heartbeat. The words are runoff gibberish. A scrabbling coral bounces on each syllable where the subtitles invade the screen.

The viewer prays along. Nudity is encouraged.

Adrasteia martyr. Adrasteia fruit cup. Adrasteia daughter of no one. Adrasteia of the silted horde, miniscule in sea kelp. Adrasteia unheard of, zero in being, in gift of verticality, in binding with drowned thresholds, in complex spasms of water, in hidden light, in manifest light, under a shield that is not a storm. Adrasteia chewing through calcerous luminescence, bidden by endless becoming.

The giggling man chants, clothed in someone else's skin. Adrasteia extrudes her new teeth in the shape of a key. She hides it from her captors under the sluggish pinprick of her tongue. The problem with a plot about kids recovering from being sex trafficked is that there are no kids, only traffic. Pedestrians win you ten points apiece. Stealing a police car gets you five stars. Looting boosts health. If Adrasteia breaks character and whispers in the policeman's ear that she's been kidnapped, he will not hear her. She lacks the cognitive framework to formulate the lines in the correct semantic sequence.

Adrasteia passes the policeman, leaking fluids from her severed neck. The cop is as much help as a preacher, less than a towel. Too much shame for sunlight. Too much sound for a spliced journey. Her lips split, unsure if their restructured shape is the result of a shipwreck or a car crash, unsure how to emit an explanation of what's wrong with the conceptual arc of this disordered plot. After all, she's a child, not a fucking script doctor.

The cop retches away in disgust. The viewer suppresses a guilty laugh.

Adrasteia's head drifts to the bottom of a sea with no floor, plunging to unending depths. Her hair spins in slow motion, circling her head like a nest. Her eyes remain wide. A single bubble escapes her razor-cropped mouth and takes the opposite path to the surface.

Top equals darkness. Silence equals death. The viewer offers patronizing advice, hand on Adrasteia's thigh, hiding under the camouflage of the giggling man's skin. "Never trust the cops. They'll haul you in and take your money. Relax. Be yourself."

Short of being allowed to take a shower, Adrasteia won't experience the privacy required to learn to act natural and be herself, especially with a stranger's hand stroking her thigh. Who her self is supposed to be depends on an underground world where people are treated like meat and you walk through your life as if none of this is happening, as if your children are safe. The problem with making a snuff film is that there's only one way it can end. Pornography in general suffers from a similar ritualistic crux. Adrasteia is running out of options while you watch the film in your comfortable chair as if none of this is real, as if none of this is your problem.

The viewer communicates arousal by fondling a proxy. The giggling man stands atop the shipwrecked pyramid of bodies mangled after the impact of the first sequence. His dominance is alluring to the audience. His crotch reeks of motor oil. He rumbles like a balloon, which is to say, he squeaks.

The narrative arc swings back and forth through time with absurd abandon. Adrasteia's oracular constriction reads as deliberate ignorance, unforgivable in a sacrificial hostage. The men round up more razorblades to hollow out the rest of her and scrape her carapace clean. The soaked terrain provides a palisade where Adrasteia is forced to ride.

Floating at the surface of the set with barely enough water to breathe, Adrasteia eyes the ignition between slashes of the giggling man's camera moves. The wrecked vehicle steams. Her tongue licks her heated key. Adrasteia wishes herself small enough to squeeze into the space between lapsed frames. In the flicker of incandescent bulb knives, she could blink out and be gone.

Flawed, she corrupts each darting chance with doubt. The location isn't familiar, so Adrasteia doesn't know where to exit the set. She tries parsing it out through the oppressive narration, unheard like a murmur on her shell. Statements carved in blood tattoos bore deeper as they fade. A show of ownership internalized. Proof of the rumor mill hangs like a stone piercing her genital plate. Every suggestion makes cracks. Silent chemical signals. Death by a thousand cuts.

The giggling man snatches the key Adrasteia formed out of her anatomy. Adds it to his toolbox. It's never seen again.

Voice-over in red.

"There's no point in running anyway because shit happens and then you die. Or shit gets real, and then you live. The key is that it's all shit."

Her tongue like a lantern, silent, lighted for fog. Divinatory shapes expelled, read fast like hot intestines. Adrasteia makes prophecy under the surface of its prongs, without protest. She grows a mastectomy long enough to blur through an underground glen and blot out all the fronds curling in the underwater crevasse. Deeper into the journey, swallowing a sea cave hollowed out in steel where hide her stablemates, Adrasteia reaches for fattened tankers rolling on the ocean floor. Sisters in poison, slender at sea level, whispering curses of sea urchins.

"You are your body. You cannot escape."

As foreshadowed in the opening moments, Adrasteia shudders, ageless, elegiac, and unclothed. Her heart beats loud and wet like Leviathan pounding the tides. Slithering strokes like sneaking footsteps swath an endless interim with sheets of panic pulled tight. In this place, where she's sharpened by scraping, the light itself is darkness. Adrasteia glows, shaved thin enough to allow light through, strong enough to keep the air out. Her dim aquatic hole where the dead go to hide.

The cave walls leak like a syphilitic prick. Her voice-over sisters spit bones, sticky tendrils, eruptions of salt. "It's best to stay intoxicated. There is a weakness you exude that attracts abuse.

Here, try one of these before they start in on you again."

Adrasteia reasonably concludes that this is all her fault. She needs to cauterize her sloppy orgasm or risk greater humiliation. The deep sea swaddles her erotically. The heart of a child snuff film is an exploration of the death of God. The giggling man has prepared an inventory of tools for the denouement. The special edition disc set comes with a list of his devices and how he uses them in each clip. Commentators speculate that he's the one talking when the viewer next listens in greedily on Adrasteia's secret voice.

"You are not a ghost, even when you try to be."

The disjointed narration struggles to impose theatrical order in the absence of plot continuity. Questions remain around the origin of the text.

"This nightmare is brought to you by assembly required."

"You can't speak. You can't escape."

The voice-over fails to intensify the viewer's arousal. Alienation from the victim is subverted by the awkward use of second person verb tense. The voice-over fails on all fronts.

"There are fissures in the—look, just trust me on this, okay? There are fissures, ha ha, and fishers of men. You are not a stone, no matter how fast you sink. Pay attention. You will remember all of this, whether you live or not."

The giggling man is taking Adrasteia apart one razorblade at a time. The intense pleasure of this experience is more confusing to her than the gnawing fear that things can only get worse. She'd hate her body for its erotic response if she believed it was still alive. Adrasteia is glad that she was never born, so she has nothing to remember. She won't have to figure out what to say regarding her role in the corruption of minors when the interviewer for the special features accuses her of complicity as an adult.

Adrasteia chooses silence. Silence is an absence of light.

When he's done deconstructing, Adrasteia allows the giggling man to rebuild her because there's no one else left. There never was. The wet, greasy muscles of the people posing like mannequins in the position of a car crash or shipwreck have failed to successfully ignite. The giggling man like a charioteer rides loud and golden above. He gestures in bone. Gestures in spine. Gestures in calcium carbonate. Makes a mess of everyone's skin. Adrasteia's new skeleton is made of razorblades and tempered hornlight. Broken windshield wipers beat a festive, irregular dirge. Adrasteia feels nostalgia. She was once a girl with a heartbeat.

Here she goes. It's time. Here's where Adrasteia makes her entrance on the set, but really, the set comes to her, as the earth hurls dirt at the windshield, and the ocean rushes in to swallow her face. Entertainment is the priority in her long-delayed execution, and it's hard to say a safe word with a mouth made of salt. Adrasteia is silence. Silence is ambergris.

The giggling man goes quiet. Adrasteia is wet. She listens for sirens but help never comes. The mermaids are strangled and hung up like meat. Her escape efforts drown. The car won't start. The set is closed. The giggling man is ready. She's a leak he can fix.

Adrasteia, in character, refuses to speak. The film is silent. Nudity blares. Her tongue like a lantern; prayer is silent. It's Adrasteia's moment to turn over and ignite. The clicking of cameras. Of posthumous tools. Of glassy events. Of oracular lamps. Of noduled tests. Of untapped venom. Of pentamerous teeth. Of steel, of coral, of underground mountains. Of holes.

The room has no windows. The set has no lights. The room is outside.

The film is a black screen with no sound. When the men find what's inside, they leave Adrasteia for dead. Her last words flash on the screen. She can't hear them because the film is silent. She can't hear them because they were never said.

Her tongue like a lamp ruled by darkness. Journeying inward, where feeling is the opposite of being. Of those beings ruled by matter, doomed to skin. Her inexpert beheading is a finite event from which she will recover. The soul never forgets. This light, in her coming, beats and comes again. The beat is with Adrasteia. Her light walks upon the face of the deep.

The light flattened on a black screen. The light locked in a basement. The light kidnapped and fucked hard and taken to Denny's for breakfast. The light grown indifferent. The light doesn't know how to save us. It can only give us more interesting STDs. The light in her mouth like a virus, inflamed by the sound of the beat.

Adrasteia, ancient, recalling a film that never was seen. The viewer will root for the maniac. while she, the silent final girl, the final light, swims in black circles around the mass death of a coral reef. Submerged, she'll live more than one hundred years. Regenerating lost and damaged parts, replacing fingers and spines, vibrating with the slow refusal of heroic life, the underwater footage of her famed alternate ending has survived.

In the restored coda, the shell's decoration of scars beautifies a body discarded as wreckage. Long thought extinct, the siren defies environmental disaster. The viewer sighs, and whether this sound signifies disappointment or relief is the test of their entrance into the myth.

Extending this lantern like hope over death, Adrasteia opens the spiny gates of her complex, reborn orifice. In vocalizations vulnerable across unknown regions of distress, in sharing the scrape of sentiment times zero times five, the eleven worlds birthed from the carcass of Adrasteia come alive too sharp to stay focused for more than a single eon. The viewer's screen is bleached with blackness. The child's last mistake is being born. Adrasteia argues, spewing kelp and sperm and salty bones. On the set, the light is darkness. Inside, there is no exit. Outside, above the water's surface, the sound of traffic is louder than God.

Rust Belt Requiescat

Ashes, ashes, Joan is in the ashes. We played the game in seventh grade. A candle or match held in front of a mirror, chanting until it lit up, a single flame in the dark. *Bones burned twice bring wishes to life*. The one time I saw it work, Tom played prelate. His bic lighter flared without a click, and a face appeared in the mirror. It wasn't the saint. It was Tom's face, old and distorted by flames.

I made my wish anyway. Tom was beautiful. I wanted to tell him how I felt.

Wishing gave me the strength to be bold. Tom told me about the bones, as if I didn't need the job. As if I needed convincing to spend the long day alone with him.

Secrets below an old warehouse: weeds in need of cutting, glass in need of sweeping, a city half brand new and half in need. I came from the needy side. All I wanted from summer was to stop wishing and stop keeping secrets. Ditch my parents, ditch this town, and make it out of high school alive.

Tom swept up while I cut down weeds. A bone in the dense brush dented my clippers. I held it up in the neon blare of sunset and we joked that it was hers. We slapped the late summer bloodsuckers that woke up to feed on us, raced each other up the spiral ramp of the empty parking garage, and looked out at Époque Isle from the warehouse roof. Across the river, casinos winked, anticipating dusk.

Tom hopped on an outer ledge and dangled his feet. No

fear of heights, as though he had wings. I imagined him soaring predatory over the river. He finished his beer and aimed the empty can at a car on rims across the street. "That magic junk I told you about in the cellar is from France. Jars and shit with weird labels."

"Can you read it any?"

"I can pronounce it, sure."

"You know what it says though?"

"Do I look like an idiot? I can figure it out." Tom stretched. I feared he might fall, or launch, or vanish like an owl in the approaching dusk. His lean body twisted, shirtless and dew-streaked in the heat. Like I said, I was done with wishing.

"Dude, you look super-hot like that."

Tom swung around and stared at me. But he didn't laugh. He didn't throw a punch.

I held his gaze, elated, fearful, trying to play it cool. "So, uh, show me these bones you keep talking up."

Maybe he smiled. It was hard to tell in the shadowy parking garage. "You're sure?"

"I don't care if it stinks. You've been down there plenty."

"Toss me another one."

I pulled a can loose from the plastic rings destined to strangle the sea life in our future. I cracked the tab, took a long first swig, and handed the beer to Tom. He drank from it, holding my gaze. We walked back down the spiral ramp, passing the can back and forth, fingers brushing, sharing our spit.

Several windows around the circumference of the warehouse were shattered. Other buildings nearby stared down at us with empty eyes. We'd bagged liquor bottles and animal droppings, cut back the massive weeds encroaching from a disused playground, and planned to board up the windows last since they allowed some ventilation. The job was bigger than we thought and now it was getting dark. The sinking summer sun sent tunnels of light through the warm air inside the ground floor. We walked through shafts of alternating light and dark. Dust particles shimmered, illuminating the invisible, as if the warehouse revealed the atoms around us that make up empty space.

A metal door barred the way to the sublevel and furnace. We weren't supposed to go down there, but Tom had all the keys. Maybe his mom thought the odor would keep him from getting curious, or maybe she was careless. Tom had made remarks more than once about how much she liked to drink.

He cracked the door, and a dead chemical barbecue smell slammed me in the face. A ladder led downward instead of a set of stairs. Tom went down first. The rickety wood swayed and snapped with every step. When it was my turn, I almost chickened out.

Tense all over and wondering how we'd get out of the hole if the rickety thing splintered, I climbed down. The close earthen walls wiped grime on my shirt. Two feet short of the floor, the ladder stopped.

I dropped onto a dirt floor.

Tom nudged me, grinning. "Cool, right?"

Breathing in dust and blinking to adjust to the dim light, I didn't want to admit the place kind of gave me a panic attack. I wanted to be close to Tom, but not this close.

Not buried alive.

From the rafters, curtains of cobwebs draped over a table staged for an antique science class. Glass tubes, beakers in strange sizes and shapes, ornate metal clamps, candles, potions, mortar and pestle, and a huge brass counterbalance scale. Piled on the end of the table, crumbling papers and moldering books steamed as the clash of summer heat and underground damp pulled rotten vapor from the teetering stack.

Wooden shelves lined the dirt walls. They were loaded with jars, tattered cloth sacks, and worm-eaten crates. The jars beguiled my curiosity with mysterious contents. Liquids, powders, and rocks: muted colors behind misted glass. Dust caked the clutter. My nostrils hitched. My throat felt thick. Even if I spoke French, I wouldn't be able to make out the labels beneath the filth.

I cleared my throat from physical need as much as anxiety. "Wow. This is wild. So where are the bones?"

Tom didn't speak. He disappeared. An unwelcome magic

trick. Then his disembodied voice drew me through an opening, almost invisible until I entered. An alcove cramped at an odd angle, hidden between the wooden shelves.

Through the alcove, I picked my way over ripped cloth and scattered bones. The tunnel terminated in the mouth of a gaping furnace blackened by old embers. It loomed like a medieval mouth of hell, big enough to swallow us whole. From its direction I caught a whiff of outside air, a relief from the oppressive smell of acrid ash.

The cold floor chilled me through the soles of my sneakers even though it was hot outside. Tom knelt and shuddered, still shirtless after working in the heat all day. "An animal must have come in through the flue," he said. He placed the bones on a ravaged linen shroud, assembling a rough model of a human form. "Thing was shut tight last I checked. I guess if they get hungry enough."

I picked up a charred sliver of bone. Maybe part of a finger. "How do you know for sure it's her?"

"The box missing on that bottom shelf."

"There's nothing there."

"Duh, I said it's missing. I worked out what ought to be there from the apothecary catalogues, found this all over the floor."

Tom touched the bones as if picking through sharp glass, or as if cleaning baby birds. His fingers trickled over the desiccated remains. I imagined Tom turning the tainted pages of the mildewed books to study the contents of the grave-like cellar and blackened furnace room. The thought of those same fingers on my skin made me cringe.

Reverence altered Tom's voice. His tone sounded deeper. "Once I have her organized, only a few simple steps remain."

"It's not her. Can't be."

"You calling me a liar?"

"Not you, the creeps who dug this hole. I googled it: someone said they found her in France a few years ago. The government or something did tests. It was a hoax. Nothing but ground up mummy rags and cat bones."

Tom rose and faced me with one hand on his hip. I'd never seen him stand like that, kind of girlish. "My great-great-grandfather dug this hole. Our ancestor rescued the bones from destruction hundreds of years before that. We risked the question of the Inquisition to save her. Does that sound like a hoax?"

"Dude, sorry. I didn't mean anything."

Tom closed the small distance between us and cupped my shoulder. His hand felt clammy. He stroked the side of my neck. A bad smell like damp, raw meat slid over me as he spoke.

"It's not important for you to be smart. Only willing."

"Willing to what?"

"Trust me. As simple as that."

His whisper sickened me. Close enough to kiss, Tom's jaw and upper lip showed a blueish shadow of beard I hadn't seen in the daylight. The underground illumination must have disoriented me with its weird shadows. Maybe I was overreacting to the tight space. I felt confused. After months of crushing on Tom, all I wanted was to make him back off.

I tried to keep it casual. "Yeah, sure thing, man. You know I do."

Tom pressed my shoulder in a quick caress and released me. Relief allowed air back into my lungs. He left the alcove to set to work with the ancient chemistry set.

I squeezed out after Tom in a nervous haze, trying to reconcile how my eyes were showing me he'd visibly aged. Bulging knuckles sprouted where once Tom had smooth, strong hands. Craggy fingers ground yellow chunks into powder. From clipped spiral tubing to a configuration of suspended globes, he transferred liquids to and from beakers on the brass scale. His fingernails lengthened. The bizarre wizard impersonating Tom placed metal weights on the opposite hanging tray until it balanced.

I stared. My mouth was probably hanging open like a jerk.

Tom's face was cloaked in shadow. He whispered orders in the altered voice. "Light the furnace and tend the flame to a severe heat. Hurry, time presses us."

I didn't know what to do. I wanted to bolt up the ladder.

I was close enough to make it. If I went to the furnace, I'd be trapped in the hidden alcove until Tom allowed me to pass. I wasn't sure how easy that would be. I wasn't sure what was happening to Tom.

Eyes glinted from the blackness. "You needn't be brave to raise the dead. I have enough courage for us both." The glint vanished as Tom spun and grasped a container from a high shelf behind him. I recognized the lean stretch of healthy muscle in his back, the blush of sunburn brightening his shoulders, the familiar nape of his neck.

I shook the crazy thoughts out of my head and ducked into the alcove.

The lever for the flue screeched like a tortured bird when I yanked it down. I piled wood and scrap for kindling in the ashen pit. The mouth of hell welcomed me: I didn't need to stoop to come and go from the massive chamber. I lit the kindling at the outer edges of the pyre in three places and shoved my lighter back in my pocket. My knuckle scraped something hard, and I pulled out the object that drew blood. It was the shard of bone I'd picked up from the ground floor of the warehouse.

I sucked the scratch on my knuckle clean and pushed the shard deep in my pocket.

Light flashed behind me. I turned towards Tom. Slurry in a globe-shaped beaker glowed vivid lapis blue. Clamped above a candle, a glass spiral tube connected with a larger globe where beads of clear liquid dripped. While the extraction progressed, Tom unlatched a small, carved box he'd placed beside the books. He lifted out strips of scorched fabric.

Heat from the furnace called my attention back to my task. I found a leather bellows to breathe life into the fire, pumped the wooden handles, worked up a sweat, and adjusted the blaze with a long cast iron poker. Warmth didn't cheer the damp, underground chamber. Flickering shadows darted from the mouth of the furnace, slathering the walls with fierce heat. Flames tasted every surface. Glowing tongues licked my eyes dry. Panting, I stumbled over Tom's clothes outside the hidden alcove. His belt snaked through the loops of his discarded jeans. The buckle clattered under my feet.

When I looked up, Tom blew out a candle.

The lapis liquid had solidified into a crystalline powder. Draped in the charred rags he'd removed from the elegant box, Tom looked like a tenant of a grave. The smell of old ash and new burning dust mixed with his strange body odor, once so erotic and intoxicating to me. Tom's fragrance was foul, as if the decomposed fabric had infected him with its decay. I stayed as far away from him as the precarious shelves surrounding the tight space allowed.

Shrouded in ancient rags, Tom unclamped the globe-shaped beaker. A crooked hand shook the iridescent powder inside. Tom's face remained eclipsed. His whisper was a spider crawling into my ear. "From here forward, neither aid nor hinder. Resist the need to intervene. An incorrect gesture may cause great harm. Do you consent?"

I nodded. What else could I do? The room keeled. My legs buckled. Unsteady against the churning heat from the furnace and Tom's overwhelming stench of decay, nausea funneled me down to my knees.

Tom crouched beside me. The bones lay before us on their tattered linen. Tom poured the blue substance into his palm and cast powder over the bones with five flicks of his wrist. Unintelligible conjurings crept through my ears as if a spider laid eggs in my brain. The weight of the air and the ripe smell of disintegrating flesh forced my head to the floor.

My temples pulsed with eggs eager to hatch, ideas seeking to breed, a backwards church building a fever cathedral inside the porous membrane of my skull.

Tom turned and smashed the empty globe with a sharp shout. He dropped the glass that remained in his fist and folded the ancient, stained linen around the legendary bones. Lifting the wrapped remains, he cradled them and carried them to the furnace.

By the time I understood—

I'd dreamt all summer of a terrible, unthinkable thing. I remembered the helplessness of the dream, but not the thing itself. In my nightmare, every objection congealed in my throat. I existed out of sync, trapped in slow-motion. By the time I garbled out a protest, it was too late to make it stop. The terrible thing happened.

This was the terrible, unthinkable thing.

With the bones swaddled in his arms, Tom walked into the furnace and caught fire.

The shocking smell of human flesh triggered a primal alarm. My mind blared. I flew across the dirt, grabbing vials and jars and anything fluid to douse the fire. Holy Christ, Tom was on fire. His black silhouette blazed in bizarre silence. He should be screaming: why didn't he scream? He should be shrieking and howling as I howled and shrieked, not silent and somber and hooded by blue flame.

I braced the flue lever with my shoulder and shoved. Halfway up, it stuck. The room flooded with smoke. The fire dulled, but not enough. Not enough to stop the sizzle of flesh. Not enough to starve the hungry blaze of the oxygen that made it rage. Only enough to stifle me and consign my carcass to the dirt.

I choked and crawled. The ladder, the ladder.

Then the mouth of hell flared. A sulfurous blast vomited up a taste of tortures to come. My vision fluttered black and bright, on and off, as billowing wings of heat rescinded in the glare. Beating a defense against the departing smoke, my heart and lungs convulsed. The furnace inhaled the thick, toxic air, and I breathed in regal fragrances of bergamot and amber.

From the throat of the fire, a figure emerged.

Dressed in white, a man carried a child draped across his arms. His pristine clothes remained untouched by the blackened furnace or the steady flames. Theatrically out of date, thick woolen hose replaced pants, an embroidered doublet covered his chest, and a sickle of pure white fur framed the top of his cloak like a precarious nest. His face perched like a bird of prey.

It was Tom's face. Not Tom in real life, but a caricature of Tom. Hair so black it shone blue. Chiseled onyx beard. The sharp point of the beard sliced into the fur collar. I envisioned the blood of the animal killed for his vanity staining the pure white pelt with warm red drops. Instead of blood, cold tears collected like ice on the lifeless fur.

"Pity me, dear maid, and awake."

The child in his arms was dead.

"The blackening, the whitening, and the reddening, by my will. This is the great work." He turned to me. "Are you prepared to do your part?"

I stared at the child, not quite a child: an adolescent girl in leather armor.

"Answer."

I cowered. I shook my head, shuddered at Tom's costumed face.

"You came here willingly. I used no force."

The plump part of Tom's lip repulsed me with a quivering pout. I'd craved his mouth for months, years. Wished for that tender part of him to touch me and bless my skin. Now it was a terse thread binding me with an army of curses.

"I don't understand. I don't want to die."

Tom's lip hardened into marble. He cornered me with another man's eyes, eyes full of laughing ice. "What do you see when you look at me? I am a child of God, the same as you. I approach you in my full truth."

The bone shard in my pocket stabbed my hip. The pain spoke, enlightened me, prodded me to gaze rather than grovel. When I dared look at the stranger in Tom's body, an encyclopedia of images opened in my mind.

The man was several centuries old. He invited me to know him.

"Turn not away," he said.

Three hundred severed heads in numerous stages of decay lined the bedchamber walls of his palace: all children, all murdered, all loved. He selected one to take down and fondle. Hours of lascivious meditation built an emotional grotto inside him, a hidden temple of lust devoid of logic and impervious to time.

A baby appeared elsewhere, slathered in blood. A natural birth. Nature's fuel is blood. As an older boy, torn open by his uncle, the boy left to savor the taste of blood alone. If the boy didn't stand and fight, he lost the game. He had no father, no mother, only the game that taught him love was a sword. Trained for the competition of men with swords, with crosses, with flashing phallic signs of transcendental madness reared in battle at full gallop, the boy exceeded his uncle-sadist as he amassed his army. Inside each soul a cistern of gore filled to the brim, spilling over, welling up from the misunderstood hearts of men to wash the land in the blood of fathers, sons, enemies, and brothers.

In battle, their blood was one color.

The man, the monster inside Tom, deepened his grotto to dam the flow, a sacred reservoir. His cistern filled and kept filling. He embraced hundreds in death, delighted in their passing, and mourned none but his own infant soul.

Recognition lit up in Tom's eyes. "She saw as much and more. She knew me. She will behold me again on this, her resurrection day."

A black pit emptied my stomach. I convulsed to let the bile out. My vomit smelled like ash. The murderer's attention went to the body in his arms, the coagulation of fire that had yet to take her first breath. "My sole spiritual compatriot. My maiden. We two alone know of conversation with angels: she in the airy heights of her magnificent innocence, and me in the true bible of the human body."

"You're a murderer."

"Is it murder to unleash raw wings from purest flesh?"

The shard in my pocket sharpened my fear-clouded thoughts as it pierced my skin. "What gives you the right to bring her back? What makes you think that's what she wants?"

My words surprised me. The thing using Tom as a puppet engaged my argument with the pleasure of a seduction. "All mortals seek eternal life. To deny this is blasphemy. Do you negate the truth of heaven?"

My pocket was damp. The shard drew blood. "Shut up, freak. I need to speak to Tom."

"We are speaking."

"Listen, I'm talking to Tom. Let's get out of here."

"I am he."

"Dude, seriously. Have you ever talked like that? Can you even hear yourself?"

"As you observe, I am somewhat changed." The eyes imitating Tom flickered. "I shall not hinder your flight. If not you, others abound."

My jealousy flared. "What others?"

"Others who dare not speak for a saint. Be off, hypocrite."

I stood to grab the ladder and doubled over instead. The shard had worked its way into my hip. I rammed my fingers through the ripped pocket to fish it out. I couldn't find the break in my skin. I tore at my jeans, jamming the zipper. There was no wound, yet the bone stabbed in the cradle of my thigh. Tom's eyes darted from my fumbling hands to the girl in his arms and then wisely back.

When I looked up again, the girl was on the ground. Tom's forearm hooked my neck from behind, and he grabbed me between the legs. He frisked and hit the embedded shard. I screamed.

"Inside you? You ignorant, blasphemous child."

Dragging me back from the ladder, he hurled me onto the dirt. My head hit a low, dusty shelf. Vials smashed and spilled, staining me with strange tinctures. Tom dug his knee into my chest, covered my mouth and nose with one strong hand, and ripped into my thigh with a blade snatched from the ceremonial wooden table.

The stab of the knife sent me beyond pain. The cool blade dissected my warm muscle. It cancelled all my normal sensations. Smothering in shock, my blood left my body in slow motion, like a tedious silent film. Rich red puddled on the hardpan dirt forming round, trembling edges. When liquid broke free, crimson spread across the cellar. Blood sprayed upward from my groin, re-enacting an animal sacrifice and spattering Tom's white fur cloak.

I was nothing to him, less than an animal, fodder to fill the cistern that stretched across time through the murderous soul of Tom's puppeteer. Like all the others, I was a willing victim, a child, a plaything.

He excavated in search of the shard, goring my limp body.

Unsuccessful and enraged, he dropped the knife and tugged my thigh open with both hands. My free jaw yawned in the shape of a wail. I didn't hear my voice, didn't have control of the slack, pliable thing that represented my body. Somewhere outside of it, a man fingered my pelvic bone. Black words exited his mouth. Phrases formed like ripening fruits that dropped from his marble lips and rotted before they hit the ground. They piled high, soft skins ripe with moldy fur that disintegrated into black liquid sugar. Thirsty creatures with pestilent wings fluttered from the furnace alcove to alight and ingest the sludge. Fighting one another and flapping like diseased bats, the rabid shadows scattered my blood across the dirt as they fed. The red splatter reached the girl's corpse.

Behind the artifice of Tom, behind the rapist dissecting my thigh, behind the shadow-creatures drunk on the words of his vile curses, the inert form of the girl awoke.

She startled first, and gaped at her bloody fingertips as if bitten. She gazed up, met my eye, and with no hint of hesitation, rushed into the scuffle between us.

She shoved Tom off of me, catching the puppeteer off balance by surprise. The winged beasts ceased feeding and darted back into their hidden niche beyond the furnace. Tom came back at the girl with teeth and recovered knife, the angry reflex of an animal. She grabbed the hilt of her sword and Tom glimpsed her face. He dropped his weapon, crossed himself, and fell at her feet.

Her sword hand hovered. Her brow creased. She took in the bloody pit, my mangled thigh, and Tom's prayerful bow. "Milord, is this Hell?"

Tom's puppeteer raised his bearded face. A smile suppurated on his lips. "No, it is not, for I have saved you from death. Behold, my dear maid, this place is your birthing chamber within the wholesome earth."

The lines deepened on her brow. "This sorcery is late. In Rouen, you left me to the prison guards and curious nobles. I am no maid."

"You remain a maiden to me always."

"They received many bribes, made a long game of bargaining to be first. I lost count of my forceful suitors when I realized you had forsaken me."

"What do I care if men defiled you in the natural way? I worship you. I worship the unnatural, the impossible. I alone have held your breast pierced in battle. Twice did I save your life. Those wounds led not deep enough nor persisted when you flew from the tower demanding death. Your immaculate flesh healed. I stayed my retinue for your glory, though I had thrown away my devil's fortune assembling a new army for you."

The light of adoration in his black eyes did not impress her. "You abandoned me to the flames."

"Yes."

"To what end?"

"Our everlasting union as saints. Fire binds our souls."

The girl's chin tilted up. "My soul is the property of Him who succors and sustains it. It is not mine to give, nor yours to claim through vain offers of love."

"Not love. We are greater than love, beyond immortality now. We exist like divine creatures between threads of time that I weave and unweave at will. My need of this vessel to retrieve you from interment was most unfortunate. Soon, we dispense of such luggage."

Tom reached out. She drew her sword against him. He retracted his hands, placed his palms together, and pressed his fingertips to his lips. Wary of false supplication, the girl released each word with calm persistence, a freshwater river of clarity certain of its course. "I have no love in my heart when I gaze in your eyes, Milord. Our first touch razed me with terror. I asked my angels—true angels, not mongrel beasts such as you manufacture through your art—why? Why must I look into the abyss of this demonic soul and witness black, bloody, infernal things which I am helpless to comprehend? And witnessing, must I not act?"

Tom took a breath as if to answer. She did not allow his interruption and spoke in a strong voice. "My angels bade me to keep silent against my will. I obeyed, though I witnessed such obscene slaughter as I would give my life to prevent. When my maidenhood was bartered in prison, I learned of the savage pleasures men take in butchery. Yet their perversions pale against your endless rituals. Repent and be shriven, for the Savior may love you, but I love you not, Milord. I never will."

The fragment of bone in my thigh radiated a vision from her history. I saw through Joan's eyes. The day Tom's ancestor and puppeteer first brushed his lips on the back of Joan's hand in pious greeting, confused terror shot through the innocent girl's arm, through her heart, her core.

Gilles builds a cathedral from the bodies of dead children. His semen serves as glue. He practices pleasure with limbs and organs, many too mangled to name. Before death, he plays asphyxiation games with his victims and mounts them as they plead for release. He alternates between mercy and menace. The children lose their human voices and cry like animals. He glories in the animal cry. He annihilates shame in an unbearable climax. Clever, relentless shame comes back stronger after each release. Darker memories, earlier ones obscured by the lens of infant agony, defy description. Helpless to disentangle pleasure from pain, he knows no language to separate acts of love from acts of torture.

He leaves Joan to burn for his sins. He constructs a sanctuary of bones and weaves lean sinew and tense flesh through the holes. Sacrilegious magic is at work. He weaves more than meat. He weaves time. He seals himself inside, smearing soft organs as decorative manure, textured clay. He stretches skins over finished panels, stitches hairs threaded from three hundred murdered children's heads. Crowning the loft, his trophies gaze down as he elongates his cock. He bares his soul in the eye of a shredded anus, displays his gore-caked face suckling at the teat of repentance, the amputated breast. Enwombed in the safe haven of his private massacre, Gilles dreams of rebirth.

An inexperienced and protected child prodigy, Joan saw this puzzle of masturbation in a flash, with one touch.

Infected by her shard of bone, I knew that by the time she stood trial, she'd lost her psychic gift. She was powerless to apply it to her own plight. The present moment was a page torn from an unreadable book to her, a fragment out of context. Even now, reborn, she lacked the gift of vision imparted to me by the relic of her body contained in my wound.

Tom's puppeteer dared her sword and exposed his chest. "We'll burn again. I choose for us. I ordered my men to stand down and leave you to the flames. I incurred wrath and confessed to false accusations to anticipate our shared fate. Did I lie? No, I spoke the truth, and all beauty bared its neck willingly, as I do now. All beautiful boys bared their flesh. I am a prince. A sow of your base nature knows nothing of the divine."

I launched at them with my uninjured leg and hurled against Joan before she thrust her sword. We crashed into the wall, bringing down bottles and dust. Shelves and debris clattered around us. In the chaos, I rolled Joan and me into the hidden alcove near the furnace to stop her assault.

"Don't fight it. You'll kill Tom and set that monster free."

She shoved me away.

I collapsed and closed my eyes, exhausted and resigned to expire. Something warm prodded my thigh muscle apart. Her hand searched my wound. Nausea washed over me yet again. Her finger met the bone fragment. Pain made it unbearable for me to breathe.

Tom's puppeteer wavered, blocked by doubt more than debris. Joan winced at our comingled pain. We shared a brief vision, as if her gift flared up once more like the last spark of a dying fire. She removed her hand, placed it over my leg, and held firm as the wound sealed closed with the bone shard still embedded in my thigh.

"Use my strength," she said. "Take my gift."

Her steady voice broke. Her face twisted in fear. She wasn't afraid of Tom, or the thing that possessed him. She was afraid of what we both knew she had to do to break his spell.

She was only a kid, after all. When she died at the stake, she was younger than me and Tom.

She leapt into the furnace.

Tom flew. I blocked. He thrashed. I clamped him in a vice grip, a human straightjacket of straining legs and arms. He yelled abuse. I yelled back. He bruised me, and I was alive again. I wasn't on the sidelines waiting to die. I was fighting for Tom. The thing inside him wheedled and cursed, spit and kicked. I gasped at each blow to my sternum, but I held on to him tight. I yelled at him to stop, he wailed he'd see me die, and we wailed and sobbed and struggled together. Tortured by the helpless agony of Joan's screams, we wrestled against the puppeteer's ploy for salvation.

When nothing but ashes remained, Tom slumped. We went down on the dirt together. Sleep or coma, he was out cold. I held him close through the night, taking comfort in his sudden tranquility, burdened by my memory of Joan's grief.

The prophet never knew she changed history. Her gift lapsed. Prevaricating at trial, her former visions crumbled like foolish lies under scrutiny. She ended as a heretic, her bones burned twice to prevent reliquary.

Tom's diaphragm emptied and filled next to me with the unconscious wisdom of ocean waves. There was water outside of this place, a river ready to soothe us if we made it out alive. My hand rose and fell on Tom's chest. His face softened in sleep. I slid away to some semblance of peace in the early morning hours before the last of the fire went out.

We woke up cold. The fire was dead. We were alive.

Awkward at first, then joyously, we found a way to warm up. My wish fulfilled.

For a long time, we didn't speak. We put the shelves back in place, cleaned up spilled potions and broken vials. We swept up ashes, dirt, and glass. No longer bearded, ancient, or deformed, Tom folded the burnt rags into their worm-eaten crate. He broke the rough silence between us after we bolted the stubborn flue. It took both of us pushing shoulder to shoulder to force it up.

Tom took a breath, wiped his brow, and looked at the dirt. "You won't tell my mom about this, will you? She'd kill me."

I met his eye, no longer shy. "Yeah, well. Mine too."

Tom embraced me. "Thanks, dude."

When he touched me, I felt it. The fire between us.

It was more than the fire of our secrets or the fire of forbidden sex. It was the fire of our longing for something more. We rose into daylight above ground like creatures freed from the grave. We were different, but the world out there was the same. The same wrecked car sat rusting on rims in the trash-strewn road. The same buildings gaped with empty eyes, broken windows shocked lidless by blight. Another derelict parking garage fence marked the relic of a playground corrupted by weeds.

Faith in the form of the shard gored my thigh as I climbed. Tom's eyes locked on mine.

He felt the same pang. We hadn't laid her to rest.

It was only a matter of time before we'd be back down there opening the furnace, laying out the bones, and lighting the fire again.

The Anatomical Christ

I. He, Him

Pregnant with pain, burning her belly, the shock of the bullet sank Aurora like an immobilizing stone. She threw votive after votive plucked from the altar. Wicks smoked out under broken glass and wax. Fire caught at the foot of the cross and ascended ankle-high in a pirouette of flaming snakes. The statue swayed with nauseous heat. Feet melted forward, as though the savior stepped, no longer aloft and indifferent in the apse.

Hyped from a night at the club, the gut-punch of the bullet didn't stop Aurora from lugging her body to safety moments ago. Most nights Queen sat out front smoking black and milds. Others the place was locked down tight and Aurora would slow to pick up the rhythm and murmurs undulating from inside. Tonight, Queen was all in white. Snorted when Aurora stuck out a twenty with a blood-sticky hand.

"Put your damn money away, girl. Get in here."

Antioch Full Baptist Assembly, scarlet chapel of miracle healing. If Aurora had ever needed healing, the moment was now.

Aurora's blood invisible inside the building, red carpet, plush and thirsty, soaking it all up; red velvet paisley wallpaper spinning patterns out of bloody handprints. The red-hot poker bored through Aurora's belly, but she looked pale in the scarlet chapel. Mortar-pale, voice smoldering hotter than the flames tasting the base of the cross, confronting Christ who did nothing, nothing at all. "Fuck you. Ain't healed shit. Let my momma die, my cousin get locked up. Big Man shoots anyone he wants, and what you ever done about any of it? You gonna come down off that cross and make it right?"

Gunshot burning in her belly, fire hissing in hostile harmony, no sirens, no votives left to hurl, no comfort in the chapel except inevitable death. Aurora pressed her fists into the bleeding hole. She wasn't ready for her final rest. Not yet. She'd burn the whole place down and take Christ with her if it came to that.

Strange, the savior carved of wax instead of wood, moving in the heat. Molded stigmata melted into reddish droplets. Static muscles warmed, wax dripped from impaling nails. Red and brown pools thickened, extinguished flames. The statue's hands and feet came free. Through smoke and tears, bitter smell of spent wicks and snuffed prayers, the man of wax approached Aurora.

Collapsed on the altar steps, bleeding out with her last breath: "Boy, you real or fake? You gonna heal me, or what?"

Likewise bleeding, the statue knelt. His seeping wounds wept subtle brown, moist slits like premenstrual vaginas in shiny waxen skin. Pale, smooth. He had a white boy's features, white boy's accent. "You are healed."

Aurora shook her head. "Not enough. This shit hurts. Oh God it hurts."

The uncrucified man shrugged and toyed with the wound in his palm, rolling a flap of skin open and closed. Aurora clenched her body and rocked. No escape from the black pain burning inside her, no relief in stillness or contortion, nowhere to move away from the hidden flame in her belly.

"Look boy, you proved your point. Gonna burn in the afterlife. I get it. Now quit playing."

The statue looked down. Drew or wrote with his finger in the thick nap of the carpet. The lines didn't keep. He tried pressing harder, and the lines were lost again. "You have the wrong idea about me. So many teachings lost, blown away by desert sand, misunderstood and mauled. Turned into lies. Let them all blow away." He looked up, almost tearful, met Aurora's eyes. "I remember the desert, the howl, the loneliness full of promises. Forty days of freedom. I want to make a deal with you. How bad do you want to make the pain go away?"

Her bleeding had stopped. She felt stronger already. "If you expect me to reform my ways, you best reform this whole damn planet. I have to earn a living."

He straightened his body, reached for his ribs, and unlatched a door cleverly constructed to provide access to the inside of his torso. Bloodless, motionless, and unconnected, models of internal organs filled his inhuman cavity. Arranged by allegorical importance rather than function, they were works of medieval medical art. He displayed his body, an imitation of living tissue. "I know what you do. I understand your work. Touch me. Take what you need."

Aurora clutched the crafted organs. The wax surfaces deceived with blended pigment that created lifelike visual texture. Despite their moist appearance, the models felt smooth, dry, and suggestively responsive, like plastic. The heart was large in proportion to the rest, burdened by love's heft. Viscera twisted in a multiplicity of passions in contrast to a spleen slight with levity. The four liquefied humors like magic potions encased in jars. Aurora rummaged through the catalogue of the perfect anatomical man.

"Shit, shit."

She dug through Christ, dumped his contents on the altar steps. Nothing for her. Someone else's deity, binary prototype imposed by hatred of female bodies who steal creation from the jealous male god. As if Jehovah cowered at His own creation, scared of being usurped. Aurora slammed the torso door shut. It bounced back open. She shoved the statue and he grabbed her wrists. His wounds leaked their false fluid onto Aurora's porous skin. Over his slick waxen surface, the reddish brown liquid beaded in trembling droplets before sliding off to less resistant hosts: her hands, her clothes, the cavity of her exposed gut.

Gunshot-blind with pain, defiant with rage, Aurora

twisted, shook the statue, wrestled against the pliant handcuffs, his fingers molded of medieval wax. "Let me go."

"Be still and know me. Have I not given you my all?"

"Ain't done nothing."

"I died."

"I'm fixing to die too."

"I gave my all, as you have given yours, and to much lesser men. For what? This is my body. Take it. Use it as more than an object of contemplation."

Faded candle smoke choked Aurora. She sputtered and coughed. "I don't know what you're talking about."

"Take this cup. In exchange, give me yours."

He curved his hand at her lips, palm up. Fluid pooled from his everbleeding hole.

Stained by his blood and by her own, by the blood of her exploded uterus and every murderous expectation that gave Aurora no way out of motherhood except a gunshot. She should never have told Big Man what she intended to do, should have taken the money and risked infection afterward. She put her tongue to the statue's musty slits and did her best, gagged at the ancient taste. No salvation in his wounds without a price.

Something grew simultaneously more sinister and sympathetic in his affect. A softening of the harsh grip, an intimate hush in his voice. "Does this relic fail you? Centuries ago I stripped away all my humanity to become divine. Restore me. Hold me not as a distant reliquary far off from the live skin that seals your sacred center. How bad do you want to end your suffering? Are you ready to make a deal?"

II. She, Her

Pulse. Rhythm of the church, the club, the ever-hungry city vein. Rocking, rolling, pulsing. Waking, Aurora alive with a hymn of transcendent psychosis. No, this was not reality. Hallelujah, this was madness.

Hanging, pulsing, a congregation swayed below her. Aurora crucified in his place. Crucified and coming, vaginas weeping, suppurating slits clenching and unclenching, woeful mouths calling his name. Bleeding with the fat wick that burned inside her with holy pain. Beyond pain, crescendo, hosanna, stop. No escape from a pleasure response like a possession. No end to liquid want.

The agony of the cross nailed her orgasm in place. The choir's song vibrated in the splinters grating Aurora's back, in the quivering prolapsed uterus bolted tight as a chastity device around her hips. She strained at the memory of his thick waxen wick, the shiny sliding organ modeled on man's ideal of man shapeshifting into a perfect fit, planting new life inside her. Aurora's own life, reborn as a sacrifice.

The gunshot fire had burned inside Aurora like a nuclear sunrise. She'd have agreed to do anything to douse the pain. She had bared herself, bending over the hard altar furniture. He'd melted into her from behind. The wooden edge under her belly made dumb intercession with the moving placenta shredded by the bullet. Desire dormant, waiting for it to end, then something awakened; holding back, unable to hold back, aching, taking, she'd lost control (oh Christ, how'd Christ learned to fuck like that?) and released in a hot rush when his blissful spittle of sperm wormed its way to unity.

Rewards of martyrdom: nerves, pores, lungs filling and thrilling in easy ecstasy. Aurora euphoric, crucified.

The choir sang Selah. Queen came up to preach.

She held a chalice below Aurora, amassing the reddish-brown drops. "We drink new wine from old wounds. The suffering of woman is invisible labor. Birth inverted, a debt never paid. Salvation is death, the end of her soul, her strength. My babies, my loved ones, all ya'll been knowing about this and playing along with this for way too long. It's time for us to rise up."

Queen lifted the chalice and invited the congregation forward. They stripped, wrapped shirts and scarves tight around their hips in homage to Aurora. The army of believers assembled at her feet. One by one, woman by woman, Queen held the chalice to waiting lips. Each kiss of the rim rippled through Aurora, butterflies in her wounds. She wept at the brush of a shy mouth, the quick lash of a greedy tongue, the immersive clasp of full lips draining and filling the cup. All drank of Aurora, and she sank beneath an ocean of mouths, prayers, demands.

Flooded, the flayed uterus girdling her heavy hips throbbed. Ripening placenta grew bulbous with weapons. Hand grenades hung like ornamental fruit, twirling and filling within the rind. Fleshy firearms formed muzzles that protruded in soft tubes, stiffened, and dropped. Meaty clusters of bullets hardening on the vine, pinkish, red-veined grapes plucked by the faithful. They pulled out a piece of Aurora's sanity with each pop. Fifty women in head scarves and loincloths traded hymnals for handguns, emptying Aurora's armory. Rage harvested, the spent placenta slumped like a tongue numb from Novocain.

Grenades before grace: a capella anthem of revolution and retribution. They marched out singing from the scarlet chapel, fifty women clad all in white, bare-breasted, and armed.

Dark in candlelight after the service, flicker, black wicks, small snakes; Aurora drunk with the erotic soup of possession, the mouths and prayers stuck on her skin. Exquisite torture, voices and needs that sucked at her most sensitive spots. The prayers never stopped. Needs, more needs. More votives and lit wicks. Eternal desperate desires. Fill one and another suckles at the same spot. No wonder Christ had gone mad.

She had only to accept symmetry, and then the swell and rush of submission brought a congregation of tongues lapping where she burned. Burn, fire, yes. Aurora needed that fire, needed that pain. Needed the sting of denial to move, to fight the nightmare of eternal suspended life.

Snapping her head to the side, harsh sting. Then harder, harder. Movement and pain. Pain devoid of martyrdom's pleasure where the stakes through her wrists ground against the joint of bone. Radius and ulna met, pinning Aurora open like a specimen, arms spread. Defenseless against gravity, fighting Newtonian laws, lungs collapsing, weight suffocating her body with each endeavored breath.

Aurora thrashed her neck. Head yanked collar bones and shoulders, internal flare like a whip. Wrist muscles and cartilage ripped. Torso sagged on shifting bones. Slight motion, gentle rocking, unequal to the violence of her pain and effort. Aurora threw her chest and knees from side to side. Ribs stabbed into heart, lungs, spleen. Impossible to breathe without hoisting her whole body up.

Stab and gasp, the cross swayed. Aurora, dizzy, no control over her landing; hurling, hoisting, stab and gasp, and again. Down, a sound like lightning. The crucifix cracked apart. Freedom. More pain. Aurora peeled the uterine tissue from her clinging skin. It shriveled and dried in the open air. Lifeless, the husk of perverse weaponry detached.

She let it go. Dropped divinity to reap hope, left the husk shedding dust on the carpeted floor. Eager to escape, Aurora preserved the presence of mind to locate Queen's collection box before she shoved out the scarlet temple's fire exit and fled through the alley.

III. They, Them

Dead Mile was the sort of club that might hire a dancer with Aurora's unusual scars, but she wasn't there for a job. Aurora buried the history of her injuries beneath her clothes. Long sleeves or sporty wrist bands, loose garments flowing around her hips, never binding, never cloying against her belly. Gowns with pockets to support her hands and wrists when nerve damage left them numb. Transitory aches radiated out from spine and shoulders, from the healed gash that striped her side, from the cavity cradled within pelvic bone. The body worked through its memories, nudging her mind with the mute sensation of screams.

A miracle she'd survived, doctors said. Aurora, unable to laugh at the irony, kept the secret of her resurrection to herself. She'd endured her miracle. She had nothing to report. It wasn't every day that a wounded woman stumbled into the ER clothed in nothing but a white and gold choir robe, shoulder dislocated, ritualistic injuries, a velvet pouch packed with cash draped around her neck. Police came, questioned. Couldn't trace the robe. Cheap polyester sold at every big box religious supply store on the strip.

Inklings of violence urged Aurora out of the hospital early. She sensed the turning tide like electricity in the air. The silent crackle before the storm. Fear penetrated her stigmata like a second coming. News of armed women in loincloths and head wraps marching on banks, churches, municipal buildings; a favorite joke on the ER's constant TV monitor until The Scarlet Woman's Liberation Army seized city hall and executed a corrupt official on livestream. If they did that, what would they do when they seized their runaway deity?

Recovery slow and strange, from hotel to hotel, never copping enough drugs, then giving up on drugs, drawn to the sacred heart of her pain. The anatomical origin. She traced his path to Dead Mile beyond the strip, edge of abandoned industrial sites. Unlit streets, graveyard of warehouses, machine scaffolds rising over flat, paved land. Aurora alone, entering an unmarked door.

Spacious; hushed voices or silence from clients clustered near the stage. Waiting, curtains closed, DJ an invisible bug under headphones, slow ambient waves. Aurora sat at the sparse bar, distant, removed from the regulars. The warehouse long and dark, lots of room between tables for perverse words, for wheelchairs, for obesity, for nonconforming bodies to move unimpeded, accepted, desired. Anything unexpected, anything you want.

Quiet, so quiet. Aurora relieved she wasn't late, not drinking her drink, no taste for it after the ER, the chapel, the ecstatic drugs of martyrdom and pain. Lights dimmed. The music changed. The doorman locked the door. No admittance once the show began.

Organ music pulsed with a sleazy undertone. Coyly, through heavy red curtains, a cross-dressed Christ slinked, toes first. Long rainbow locks, wig of many colors, wraparound mini-dress and thigh-high boots. Slow, solemn gesture of spiritus mundi, then peeling off gloves, stigmata slowly revealed. Bending to the audience, not teasing: reaching out, touching hands like Thomas, inviting fingers and tongues. Aurora uncomfortable, feeling the curious, worshipful probes like sparklers below the healed skin of her identical set of wounds.

The statue stood back dramatically, spun, and undid his sash. Spun again, mini-dress flying off, wig askew, deosil dervish twirl until dizzy, drunk, he bared his newly molded wax breasts. Fondled them with a saintly smile for the rapt audience. Turned sideways, forefinger sliding in and out of his mouth like a lewd come-on, and then traced spit on the moist lips of the gash in his side. An older patron tucked a twenty into the leaky slit, and the grey-green bill turned brown with old blood.

Aurora couldn't see the next move without coming close. Familiar feeling of wonder: door open, organs out, modeling the mystery of flesh, tactile as sex toys in the clientele's caressing hands. Aurora breathing in synchronicity, Christ in a circle of admirers, circle of touch. Shared stimulation, joy in loss. Take me. Touch me. Flesh of wax melting, morphing in the circle of human heat. Bodies surrounding Christ, using his smooth organs, alone, in pairs, in a threesome. Using, finishing, leaving. Christ writhed on the floor in money and mock guts carelessly dropped.

Aurora assembled the ravaged contents of his cavity and placed them behind the door in his chest. Having hung in tandem, she knew there were other doors further down, invisible, locked and hidden from Christ. Alone, he lacked the power to open them. Aurora closed the torso door, latched it as a mother might tuck in a sleepy child. Post-coital Christ still hummed with desire, but wary, or maybe wishing for it, he said, "Are you here for revenge?"

Pale wax skin, dirt stuck into misshapen melted parts. One breast inverted, wig off. Aurora kneeling, uncertain how to answer, picturing Christ drawing in the carpet, drawing in the sand, embodying the gap that defies violence. "Thought I was. Now I'm not so sure."

He splayed his arms wide, stigmata slapping the floor. "Have at it, honey. Do your worst. Tear me apart."

"Those folks beat me to it. How often do you do this?"

"As often as it takes."

"For what? To find meaning in suffering?"

"Suffering is as meaningless as joy. Death is my father's only gift to this world. I am his incarnation, his foolish conceit. How can an eagle teach ants to fly? If I can escape divinity for one moment, escape enlightenment for one second—but, oh, where is freedom located within this relic of false flesh?"

He clutched at the deforming wax, stretching, morphing, undoing the careful work of the medieval craftsmen who had lavished Christ with dull, innocent faith, and brought him wrestling against a mind as vast and horrible as the empty cosmos to latch behind a tiny door, a miniature compartment, cradled in needy hands, battered by greedy prayers, a thing pawed and touched and never felt, never known.

Aurora clasped his thrashing wrists. She knew him. Knew and hated him for coming down off the cross and making it hers. "You should have kept your damn divinity to yourself."

Softened hands like clubby claws struggled. She stifled them. Pulled the statue across her lap, pieta restrained by force; Aurora, gritting her teeth, spitting down on him. "I'm going to forgive you, fucker."

"Don't."

"What the hell else am I supposed to do? When Queen gets to one of us, and you know she will, she'll nail the other in place. Her revolution is the same old shit. New face, same coin. Hold up a minute; listen. Do you hear that?"

Outside, armed marchers gathered, fanatical fires expanded, crusading crowds amassed. Queen preached. Church was happening in the streets. A megaphone rattled the club's walls: "This is the dawn of a new messiah. All will share in her sacrament. Soon she will be returned unto us. She will be given."

She, Aurora, clasping her captured Christ. He, confined, face muddled in imitation of corporeal anguish. Inexpert restoration, half an artifact. Which half? Wailing: "Who owns this body? Am I nothing but an incarnation of my father's desire?"

"Not us, not yet. Incubator—"

Yelling louder, fighting against the megaphone. "Property of father, Queen, states, laws. Nothing, so much nothing. Medical model, sex toy, bastard son, drag clown, sacred whore; nothing, nothing."

Collapsed in manic laughter, malleable statue in Aurora's strong arms. Human arms, not weapons. Arms strong with impossible survival. Compassion hers to give, wisdom to open doors, necessary director of magic beneath his human costume, his obsolete striptease. Aurora ordered: "Give back what you took from me. Fuck martyrdom. Fuck suffering. Hurry, before they break down the door."

Submission, finally seeing, understanding the inherent violence. Soft voice. "Our body is a temple. Two or more gathered. Open my chest. Take it all. Tear us apart."

Trading tender pieces, constructing the world anew. Final girl and final god, one Great Beast, girded for war.

How To Fillet Angels

Steve raised his voice to cover the sound of his stomach growling. "I'm in awe of his work."

Martinique tossed her hair and clattered away, kitten heels and a deep belly laugh echoing through the empty art gallery. Steve felt he'd been tricked by her manicured tips clawing at his shirt, implying she and Steve were co-conspirators in a devious plot. He was glad she'd let go. Her talons gave him unpleasant goosebumps.

"You're a babe in the woods, darling. He simply adores his block. He's the tortured saint, martyr to the cause." She dropped a keyring on the reception desk. It was the sole disrupting element in the clean, open space that Martinique managed for her famous spouse. "Remember, anything you need goes on the INsouciance account. Smack, boys, girls, goats. I don't care what you're into. Whatever gets the work done. Opening night's in three weeks."

Steve didn't want her to think he was desperate. "I'm here to honor a great master. The work will be done as intended."

Martinique paused and tilted her head. "He was marvelous in his prime. Hungry, angry, on a crusade to devour the world. Alas, no more. This space simply screams for new life."

She gestured at the smooth, spackled walls. Steve smelled fresh gesso. It was the smell of hope. Steve's art would no longer languish in the destruction and renewal of the urban forest. INsouciance, exclusive showcase to the legendary painter Serelna, had opened its arms to welcome him home.

Martinique completed her retreat across the windowless expanse of the stark gallery. "Three weeks. I expect nothing less than a brilliant massacre. Remember, I need only choose, and behold!" Martinique's fingers splayed in a magician's gesture of revelation. "Talent becomes manifest."

She waved her dismissal and let the door slam on the way out.

Steve was alone on sacred ground. He climbed the spiral staircase that led to the residential loft. He hesitated before dropping his battered knapsack at the foot of Serelna's bed. The possessed genius must have collapsed here, enervated between bouts of inspiration. The low-ceilinged nook offered dusty sheets and empty ashtrays. No personal items except for a few old paperbacks remained. Steve tested the mattress and read the spines: *Marauder in Black. Butcher, Angel, Bride. The Black Angel's Disguise.*

Under the smell of detergent, the strong scent of a man lingered.

Steve sank into the pillow. His eyes traced a preview of his project on the ceiling, a forced daydream he employed as a preamble to beginning a new work. Part of his mind refused to cooperate, intent on reflecting back. Steve Shred's old name had died of neglect, left behind him in the suburbs. Estranged from a false female identity, Steve had fled his conservative hometown's cookie-cutter streets. Young as ten or eleven, Steve had roamed at night and imagined a mysterious black car pulling up and offering him a new home in the city. Steve's genius immediately apparent, he'd be swept away to a glamorous metropolitan life and instant acclaim.

After couch surfing for nearly a year in the city, the dream verged on coming to life. His project at INsouciance was just in time. When Steve left that morning, his buddy's wife made it clear he was not welcome back. Steve had skulked away, feeling less than human under her disapproving gaze.

A buzzer woke Steve up. He shot out of bed. He didn't know how long he'd been asleep or how long the buzzer had been ringing. If he didn't take delivery of his art supplies, he'd lose a whole day of work.

Stumbling and swinging down the spiral staircase, yanking the metal gallery door, then remembering the keyring when it didn't open, Steve yelled, "Hold on!"

The Utrecht delivery guy was a cute girl. She hadn't heard Steve's name on the art scene and openly asked who he knew. "Nobody," Steve said.

"So how'd you land such a sweet gig?"

"I sent in a proposal, like anyone else. I guess I got lucky."

"Plus mad talent, right?"

Bashful at first, Steve described his plan for the project as he helped unload the truck; the interactive and ephemeral elements, how he'd practiced rogue installations in warehouses and alleyways, evading arrest. Gaining confidence from her enthusiasm, he invited her to be his guest on opening night.

"Fuck, yeah. You can count on it."

Steve held the door for her. "Cool. See you then."

She waited. When Steve didn't make a move, her smile altered, and she stuck out her hand. Steve shook it, completing a perfect pair: both hands were calloused, short-nailed, and embedded with pigment stains. "Good to meet you, Steve Shred. You're, um, an interesting guy. See you in three weeks."

After he let go, Steve felt a jolt of terror. He'd never see her again. He had to hold on. He had to run into traffic and flag her down, beg her to stay.

He crushed the impulse. It didn't make sense, and after a year living like a bum, it was easy to imagine her admiring smile mutating into a defensive glare.

Women would look at Steve different after the opening. Everyone would. Steve wouldn't forget who had been kind and who had derided him. He'd remember his true friends after he hit it big.

Steve backed into the gallery. The security door swung shut. The automatic lock clicked. To barricade against intrusion, he clamped down the dead-bolt as well.

Steve's stomach groaned.

His empty gut twisted with familiar craving. He bent over until the pangs softened into mild nausea. He was used to the sensation. He chose meds and art supplies over meals when he couldn't afford both. He'd been too nervous to scarf down a bagel at his buddy's house this morning and hadn't eaten since last night.

Half a day already wasted, Steve gulped down enough tap water from the small service bar below the loft to quiet his gut. He selected a wide-edged brush from the glorious array he'd bought on the INsouciance account and mixed a Venetian Red wash for the first layer of roughing in. The cold undertones of the pigment suggested scarlet blood on the plate of a delectable steak, pomegranate sauce on crispy duck, or a charred burger staining a fresh white bun with flavorful pink juice after the first bite.

Steve salivated. That was fine. He'd stay hungry. Like Martinique said of his hero Serelna, he was on a crusade to devour the world.

Thinned-out pigment dripped with exacting moderation when his paint hit the wall. Steve struck harder where he wanted a wide splatter. He sketched with the bristles blotted dry for a feathery nuance and pressed the edge of a loaded brush while leaning in with variations in force to punch up the drama in the line-work. Viewers moved by the emotional impact of Steve's visuals might fail to recognize the methodical control behind his wild strokes, but a trained eye saw beneath the surface. Beauty and balance lived within the chaos. Steve's relationship with the texture, movement, mixing qualities, and drying times of paint gave him exquisite control of his medium.

Paint was the first step. As the foundation for the piece that would make or break his career, it had to be perfect. And it was. The bones of the basic structure opened up before Steve like a fiery, bloody pelvic cave carved into the wall. Cracked apart, a winged phoenix arose butchered and gored. Steve stuck the wet brush into a jar of cleaner and broke a vine of charcoal in half. The snapping sound satisfied a ritual intent. With the wide edge, Steve tinted the wet wash with the crumbling grey vine. It dimmed the fire, incinerating ash through the leaking, liquefied red. The technique teetered on the verge of creating a muddy disaster.

Steve smiled. He loved pushing a dangerous edge.

A smoke-toned skeletal horde amassed on the wall. Between glazes, Steve moved the ladder, knelt, and crossed the gallery back and forth to check every angle. He followed his borrowed mantra: *Ninety percent looking, ten percent doing.*

Great master in the making, heir of Serelna, Steve imposed his internal vision onto external reality with easy clarity while alone. No crisis of confidence unnerved him. His focus danced on a high-wire, relaxed and intense. But then, in his timeless, immersive state of flow, in the windowless, dead-bolted industrial space, an unexpected high-pitched howl ripped through the silence.

His stomach again.

The energy collapsed. The image corroded. Steve threw down his brush. His squealing intestines breached the sacred space. Visions of tender grilled meats and roasted vegetables assaulted him. Rich side dishes and fresh corn, every holiday rolled into one. His belly screamed. A relentless rat gnawed through his gut.

Steve raided the service bar for snacks. He scarfed down a handful of cocktail onions and mixed nuts. The pockets behind his molars stung with the shock of salt. After a few bites, he felt back in control of his concentration and free of cramps.

He finished off the dregs of a bottle of Chardonnay from the rack in the door of the mini-fridge. Its shelves were stacked with items wrapped in butcher paper, labeled by date. The oldest ones buried on the bottom were too smeared to read. Soggy, they leaked with something rotten inside. Steve winced and closed the door to seal away the filth. Cleaning up after the last opening party was not his job.

Pumped to get back to work, Steve surveyed his emerging masterpiece from a distance. His eyes locked on an absurd flaw. He hadn't seen it from any other angle before going behind the bar. A wide swath of paint dripped down the center of the main wall. Its thickness morphed at the bottom into the shape of an oval. At the floor, the oval cut in half. The remaining black archway looked like a cartoon mouse hole.

Steve strode across the open space and smeared out the shape with rags and thinner. He blended the edges into an amorphous shadow. Lifting as much of the pigment as possible, he sprawled flat on the floor to eradicate the stain.

Standing too fast, his vision suffered a split-second blackout.

His body felt cold and disjointed. Steve shivered at the thought of another foolish oversight marring his masterpiece. He'd made a good start. Today was a long day, an emotional day. He'd fight again tomorrow.

Pounding Serelna's pillow perfumed the loft with the rangy odor of the man. Steve inhaled, comforted by what he should find unpleasant. The absence of window apertures pleased him, also. Cordoned off from the demands of daily schedules, survival needs, and social stigma, Steve undermined all the weapons the world used to kill his creativity. Housed in Serelna's secluded gallery loft, the invisible mentor fostered him. Day and night didn't matter. The space held him. Steve had permission to follow Serelna's unique circadian rhythm and genius.

When he woke, Steve guzzled water in the shower, conscious that outside beyond the security door, the city boiled over with seductive food options. Myriad enticing choices threatened to intrude on the sacred space and break the spell.

Steve checked the service bar supplies before beginning the day's work. He portioned out pita bites and maraschino cherries. He rationed high-energy mixers and sections of garnish fruit. Martinique would return in less than three weeks. Steve had his phone in case of an emergency. He must not waste time on temptation. He flushed the keys to the building down the toilet.

His belly whined as the water swirled down the pipe. It rumbled along with the last lugubrious glug.

Steve ignored it. It was nothing but noise. He intended to live like a monk, devoted to his art.

Satisfied, Steve set to his masterpiece with a clear head. He gazed with triumph until his eyes sank again to the same mistake he'd corrected last night. Below the fiery, black-winged horde, below the arcane skeleton of the descending phoenix Steve had conjured to consume the churning charcoal masses, an almost childish flaw streaked the wall and clotted at the floor.

The edges were sharp. Instead of erasure, it looked as if Steve had painted the details of the cartoon mouse hole with a fine haired brush. From the long angle across the large gallery, the comic archway appeared three-dimensional, lovingly shaded to create the expert illusion of an impossibly long tunnel traversing the interior of the wall.

Steve dropped to his knees with turpentine to blot it out again. It was a shame to destroy such delicate work. Steve thought he recognized the mark of the master's hand. He felt a chill as if his mentor's eyes were upon him. Did the great man stoop to prank? If so, how did he come and go unseen?

No matter. In deference to Serelna, he must compose the work. Steve played counterpoint on the remaining walls and prepped canvas slats to pin and peel like strange skins on the interactive opening night. He layered time in primal beats, sculpted sustenance from the richness of creative communion with his idol. Internal pain prodded him like white noise, and he channeled the constant irritation into sharper awareness.

In defiance, his bowels were unpredictable. Goaded by his body's betrayal, Steve stabbed at his phone on the toilet, impatient for relief. His notifications showed INsouciance trending. The Utrecht delivery driver had shared Steve's supply list. She'd taken pictures. She hadn't asked his permission. Friends long dormant enthused over Steve's talent. The strength of their praise bore an inverse relationship to the length of time he'd been allowed on their couch. He trembled with a mixture of anger and vindication.

As Steve's wrists quivered, his brain registered the date stamp displayed. The phone shook out of his hands and smashed on the tile floor.

He didn't mean to throw it. But it was impossible. It read three in the morning.

Two weeks had passed.

Panic notes chimed from the shattered screen. Like an involuntary plasma donor, Steve was hooked to an IV pumping the lifeblood out of his veins, spewing it out like a geyser into the voracious, thirsty world. The phone was a traitor. Steve stood, grappling with his belt, feverish and unsteady. Idiotic blips and lights nagged him from the conniving device.

He knew what he had to do.

On the service bar, Steve centered the phone on the granite counter and used a stone cocktail muddler to pound it into small, silent, plastic shards.

He was free from the nagging, free from the cloying demands of an invasive outside world. Inside, the bones were good. The outline was there. The gesture of a master defied the restrictive limits of time. Not every space had to be filled. Not every less had to become more.

Unless it came back again.

Steve knew better than to turn his back. Yet seeing it, he still quailed and wept. He had left his masterpiece unattended, and the cartoon mouse hole had returned. With the comic glee of a childish vandal, the hand of a skilled artisan had modeled the tiny arc and shaded it to perfection in exquisite trompe l'oeil.

Steve's empty stomach squealed like the wheels of a rusty cart. The cartoon tunnel opened into a hilarious alternate reality that undermined his serious work. His deadline loomed closer than he'd realized.

The gastric chorus inside Steve grew louder as he approached the offending hole. He leaned down to inspect it, admire it, and destroy it. Digestive echoes came from within a deep cave.

The illusion of the archway was flawless. From within, metal grated against metal. Steve's intestines sang along. He hugged his knees to his chest. Rusty wheels creaked round and round. Steve rocked in dumb puzzlement. What looked like a small toy mining cart came rolling out of the mouse hole.

It came to rest in the middle of the gallery. Steve scuttled like a crab, clutching his gut. Closer, it appeared to be a miniature-sized palette with little handles on each end for pushing and pulling. Strapped on the bed of the cart, a bulbous, crimson thing sickened him.

It was red and thumping, with a lewd bouquet of tubes blooming from the top. Ventricles bulged and receded under the restraint of firm straps. Its vigorous rhythm spilled no blood, though the glistening surface looked slick and moist. Steve pressed a finger into the meaty lump. The heart thrummed against his touch in soothing answer to his erratic pulse. He slid his palm further to cover the pumping muscle, which fit under his fist. Its strong, steady pattern entranced him with delectable warmth.

It was a gift.

Careful, oh so careful, Steve unbuckled the tiny toy straps. He lifted the throbbing heart in both hands like a precious relic, transported it to the service bar, and slid it into the cavity of a polished silver hors d'oeuvre tray.

Steve sliced the pulsing heart and placed a tender portion on his tongue. The morsel's throb sent a pleasant shiver through his nerves. His stomach uncramped. His jaw tingled. Saliva flowed. Steve's teeth popped a membrane of the pulsating slice and loosed a thick, savory liquid into his throat. He swallowed, his body bathed in bliss.

The next bite was better than the last, and the next, and the next. Peace seeped through Steve's stomach lining and nourished his iron-deprived blood. It crossed his blood-brain barrier and triggered an erotic sense of fullness. Drawn to the other part of his body that naturally pulsed, Steve touched the great man inside him, rangy, raw, and too powerful to stay out of his dreams.

The work happened now, and now, and now. Or it didn't. Mentored and fed, Steve had no reason to rush and rather dwelled in contentment within the bubble of Serelna's transcendent space.

When Steve slept, which was deep and frequent, Serelna sent strange emissaries. A makeshift petting zoo in Steve's dreams housed a litter of small, frisky mammals within a low, portable enclosure. Not quite squirrels, nor puppies, nor monkeys, they toppled and chased each other, cavorting in endless play. Steve caressed their grey and brown pelts with his skeletal dream-hand. Aesthetically dull in appearance, their fur entranced Steve as the creatures tumbled through his bony fingers.

Bitterly he breakfasted on their stored carcasses, wrapped

and labeled by date in the service bar mini-fridge. There was no other choice. Steve accepted his duty and opened one packet each time he woke from the dream. Stiff, staring blindly at him with large gelatinous eyes, their soggy meat was rancid and tough. Fur clumped between Steve's teeth. Thin bones scraped and caught in his throat. Their joyful number diminished. When Steve ate the last carcass of his treasured pets, his work with Serelna was done.

Ants had invaded the refrigerator. They swarmed through the final rotten, desiccated meal and trickled over Steve's scabbed lips as he swallowed and mourned. Devoid of bliss, clutching Serelna's pillow, Steve implanted his body in the sculpted gallery space. Curled within an elaborate formation of the interactive walls, he held vigil.

When Serelna revealed himself, he looked much older in person than in photographs. His impatient blue eyes turned energy inward. Thick black hair littered with gray hung below his shoulders. He wore a utility shirt, loose and unbuttoned, exposing a slender chest, decadent with wiry muscle and sparse hair. Serelna spoke in a voice both detached and heavy with knowledge as if he were aware of regret while incapable of experiencing it. "You have to leave now."

Steve's voice was a rasp. "But I finished it. I ate all the animals."

Serelna nodded, looking down at the boy. He placed an affectionate hand on Steve's ragged skull. Steve reached out in wonder to touch the skin on Serelna's chest. It was flaky and soft and cool as a lizard's hide. Steve's fingertips throbbed with the pulse of his warm heart against the hollow cavity below the surface of Serelna's chest. He tapped the empty sternum and searched Serelna's austere eyes.

"An old shaman's trick," the master said, almost smiling.

The mouse hole passageway had grown as high as the ceiling. Behind Serelna, it now opened into an enormous archway that poured forth light. Over sensitized, Steve closed his eyes. The old man's outline burned on his retinas like an eclipse. His image spread into the fiery wings of a plunging phoenix, emulating Steve's masterpiece. Steve forced open one eye. Silhouetted black against the glare, Serelna stepped back and raised his arms in a shrug.

The silhouette said, "A man is more than his image."

Steve reached again. "Which man am I?"

The question stopped short in Steve's throat. He stumbled forth from the sculpted wall and gagged. Unable to breathe, he bent over and coughed up a small object shaped like an hourglass. He took a breath. He choked again. He pounded his clogged airway and heaved up a handful of similar hard objects. Some were flared on the ends. Others were odd puzzle-like shapes in sepia and ivory tones.

Steve's feet puddled beneath him.

Off balance, his gorge swelled with an impossible bulk. He retched and forced the end of a lengthy pillar-shaped object up his throat and out through his mouth. His eyes watered, blurring his surroundings. Saliva streaked his cheeks. He tugged the impossible protrusion past his windpipe. It slopped out in a pool of mucus. Steve's left leg deflated. He fell.

Tears dropped and his eyes cleared enough for Steve to see. Having studied anatomy, he recognized the pillar as a tibia, the smaller objects as foot bones.

Steve heaved again. Two hundred and fifty bones were expelled in a gradual, relentless process. As Steve's structure came undone, he labored like a boa constrictor in reverse. His hands folded up like old gloves. His ligaments and loose muscles piled below his erupting skeleton in a bag of unstructured skin.

Beneath the vomiting balloon of his head, a nest of bones surrounded Steve as he gaped like a baby bird. Serelna dug down between Steve's distended lips with strong hands and ripped his mandible out. Steve's head collapsed. The warped sack cinched shut with the slap of an incoherent tongue.

Serelna tossed the mandible away and kicked the bones aside. He pressed his hands into the disordered pile of convulsive flesh. As the great man molded, its writhing grew more rhythmic in response. Steve had no means to resist the artist. He joined the pulse of the endlessly cavorting creatures from his dreams, birthing beautiful animals to be devoured, moved by the perverse cadences of strange joy. Time was forever, space his true home. Steve throbbed in a compacted knot of aching clay. His core beat with desire. Serelna sculpted Steve to fit the shape of the empty cavity inside his chest and swallowed him whole.

The revival of gallery INsouciance was a huge smash. The mystery of his inexplicable disappearance bolstered Steve Shred's fame. He left behind a legend of great talent lost. Gossip fueled the publicity machine. Martinique and Serelna personally welcomed the Utrecht delivery driver on opening night. She had been the last to see him. They would not press charges, Martinique said, a bit too quietly. They simply wanted to know what Steve told her before he vanished.

The confused girl tried to bolt. Between the dense crowd and the obtuse installation environment, she couldn't find the way out. She plunged through the shifting gore of Steve's worst abomination, the section involving cell phone parts and small animal carcasses near the service bar, and ran up the spiral staircase to wait out the hectic gala in a solitary space. She'd search for an exit once she caught her breath.

As an aspiring painter eager for a break, she didn't question the ethics when Serelna appeared in the loft, offering sympathy for her plight. He suggested she participate in the next group show INsouciance organized. He'd talk to Martinique. No need to run. He seemed kind enough, not invested in veiled threats, and attractive in a ragged sort of way. She allowed the great genius to seduce her.

The bed in the loft was small. She didn't like the smell. She brought him to orgasm multiple times. He demanded more. Despite her inexperience with male partners, she did her best to endure. At least he knew what he wanted, so she didn't have to figure out how to make him happy. The old man thrust, shuddered, and gasped with ecstatic violence. She felt overcome by an army.

His body heaved. His skin quivered. Strange organs writhed like small animals underneath the surface. His sternum seemed to glow with a demon's face when he neared climax yet again. A tongue lolled out below the demon's red pleading eyes.

The delivery girl stared. The eyes pulsed. The tongue throbbed. The old man moved faster. His heart raced as if to escape his torso. He clasped her tight, and she felt the organ pounding, pounding, beating against her body, hammering at her skin, thrashing in a desperate bid to burst through his chest.

The Buried King

"Am I doing this wrong?" Dionysus wrapped in amethyst, stone threaded garments masquerading as wings of feral fishermen. Homeless by a rust-colored dumpster, the label is amethyst, regal, in a bottle with a cap the shape of a crown. Kings of cardboard booty and shameless hope fished from a river. "Boy, you better not eat them trout."

Pollution of angelfish and angelic poisons. What's an angel but a demon in agnostic disguise? The kid stalks the older man by the quayside, secluded in reeds. Seed-heads match the boy's hay-colored hair. "He's one of them angels, one of them gonna come for you, Hector. See how he's stalking? Don't look him in the eye. Don't turn."

The child alights, boy in transition, wings woven of reeds. "Gimme one of them fishes," he says.

His sepia teeth have a slime about them that shows he never learned to brush. They look too old for a child, for a boy, for most men. Most men perform wealth, whereas Dionysus Hector keeps his trap shut and picks up what tourists leave behind on the godforsaken sandbar, other side of the bay. Better fishing here under the highway, hidden in the reeds, free from sea police and starwatching dandies. In winter, he'd rather freeze.

"Gimme one, mister." The little creep creeps closer, needy beggar demon slinking in to launch an attack. Atonal fission splits Hector's decision making process. Howling in Latin, delirious in the act, for many languages have been born and died within his breast; Hector Dionysus hooks the angel-boy's lips like threading bait.

Two shocked snails hump the wire shard. Hector holds a finger up to demonstrate the virtue of silence to his catch. Angels tossed out of heaven left to rot by an obscene god too busy spinning demons out of cake mix. "Damn shame, the waste of it all," Hector says. A damned world full of damned souls, old and new, and then this kid comes along just begging for it with big eyes. Now here's a drink a man can savor.

The kid sees where Hector's looking, wants to tell him he'll do anything anyways, mister; can't and wonders how he's going to eat with his mouth hooked shut. Wonders how bad his lips are fucked up.

He can taste the blood. It's nice, really, in comparison to the brown sourness of his disintegrating gums. The man's on him, quick. Taste of metal, similar to blood.

Lepidoptera regicide, his mother ate the monarchs for their latex flavored poison. How many caterpillars does it take to get high? Being pregnant with him tasted like butterfly wings. The only thing the boy remembers she showed him is how wings turn to powder on your tongue. Killing in the name of what? Proof she didn't exist, illiterate prophecy, not one but three positions negated in worshipful posture. If you create the form, some mad god will fill it with substance. Unless they forget, too busy with the business of gospel annihilation, of seizures, of flight; they forget, and the boy learns to wait.

Hector Dionysus could be anyone from behind. The blood is nice, and the warmth of the bum's rough hands is nice. It's cold on the river. Ocean, lake, whatever. The kid accepts precedent: maenads mistaken into butterflies.

Hector sees nothing in his arms except pale white fish flesh and tangled lines. There's a Latin word for what's going to happen next. It's on the tip of his anchored tongue, a word like poisonous dust that tastes of amethyst, of crushed gems, of meaningless emotions a monster like Dionysus should have outgrown centuries ago.

He skins the fish flesh, buries it before the sea creature weaves reeds into some new camouflage, into ibis wings, into gold more precious than the ashes of kings. Hector Dionysus doubts the rave of the human encounter, attended by shredding maenads. He's left with a stomach made of sticks and a cascading gullet; a misleading sense of pride in capturing the criminal before the fall. Never trust a centaur in disguise.

Blinded by golden wings, with no other choice in battle, eyes bleed tears as he feasts. As burier of kings, Hector serves a single master, the illicit tradition of temporal decay. He cradles the long-dead angelfish in pathetic disarray.

Sympathy leeches piss from crusty eyes as veritable gospel cetology holds intent on making a raft. A cardboard casket, parts set afloat to be reassembled by goddesses. They do that, deep in the past.

Deep in the shameless hope, Dionysus craps amethyst, hides the stones he's fished from the river, wears his wings in the shape of a crown. Cardboard-colored garments masquerade in liquor. Feral fishermen keep company. Hector goes clayey with a battalion of sea police. Gullet overflowing, kids fished from the river, wanderers amass to prove the accuracy of a corrupt savior's aquatic myth:

Here is where a child washed up on shore, and here is where the drunk raped and ate his flesh, and here is where no one knew the boy went missing, and here is where the system failed. Here is the wreath of mourning tied in a chokehold of seaweed around the dead boy's throat.

For all the desires resurrected, Hector's line tugs, knocking him off balance. A big one, for water born in the ocean will bear witness only so long.

Hooked, the behemoth's mouth swells. Godly is its maw, opening unto a cavernous hell of burnished teeth. Glorious is its hunger, gorging on the liquor of the sea. Righteous is its belly, vomiting Hector Dionysus who cries out wrong and remade.

"I am vulnerable. I miss you. Am I doing this wrong?"

From lyres, the wanton sea creates kings. Noisome, they wash ashore uncrowned. An army of orphic boys with limbs rubbery and abundant as squid, their squalid sea-smell warns the slugs of approaching salt. Liquid revenge, eyes in every bottle. Amorous amethyst trout, Hector Dionysus vomits himself rightly inside out.

Peaveman`s Lament

It was all because of the snack machine.

For two weeks, the shared vending machine in Peaveman's office building had been progressively and hopelessly depleted. Chocolate bars gave way to nougat. Nougat surrendered to nuts. Nuts (unsalted) segued into expired cookies. Cookies gave up the final ghost to sugar-free breath mints and diet grape soda. Bereft, with no reasonable break time options, Mark Anthony Peaveman decided to act.

Peaveman squeezed inside the niche that housed the machine. There wasn't much room, but he was a slender guy despite his eating habits. His lithe frame gained enough traction to push. Tile screeched. The top of the machine tilted. The electrical cord snapped out of the socket like a whip. Bottom heavy with two weeks of coins, the snack machine rocked, making progress. Peaveman heaved it back and forth, lumbering it out of the alcove and to the stairwell at the East entrance. Slithering change inside the safe exaggerated the shifting weight. A can of diet grape soda broke and spat behind shatterproof glass.

The railing around the stairwell was an obstacle. Peaveman bartered the uneven weight of the overloaded machine like a lever and see-sawed it over the metal bar. Down through the hollow core of the stairwell the snack machine plummeted for eleven full flights with a soft howl of displaced air. Peaveman found it strangely lovely, like a suicidal robot taking the final plunge to its digital demise. It hit the bottom and exploded like a missile blast.

"You're my hero."

Sweaty and wild-eyed, Peaveman turned towards the voice. It was one of the new hires, one of the cookie-cutter people who came and went so frequently at the job. Looks didn't matter at the call center, an aide to Peaveman's relative success. The kid admiring him had about five piercings in their face and twice as many colors in their hair. Peaveman disdained unconventional appearances that garnered attention. He was a firm believer in flying beneath the radar. These people seemed to be everywhere lately, he thought, like some peacock army amassing to combat tasteful tones and unmarred skin. He never knew which ones were boys and which ones were girls. He didn't understand why they made it so hard for people to figure out. He was at the point in his life where he wanted all of them, everyone, peacock or not, to leave him alone.

"Come on," the kid said. "You better book."

Shouts and footfalls flooded the stairwell. Peaveman agreed with the tug on his sleeve and followed the kid up three flights to an exit. The sign on the door read "Rooftop—Restricted Area—Do Not Enter." Peaveman had never tried the door. In all his years at the job, he'd often wished to, imagining the dizzying liberation of the view high above the grind of everyday life. But the doorway was restricted. He'd always assumed it was locked.

The kid flew through with the grace of a hawk.

Peaveman limped up, aided by the bannister. He'd bruised his knee battling with the snack machine, and he wasn't very limber after ages cramped in a cubicle. A few steps above, the kid's walk worried him into awkward pauses during his ascent. Their irregular, snaking gait seemed cleverly designed to trap Peaveman's nose between butt-cheeks. The unavoidable fragrance coming from the kid wasn't the usual eau de rotten patchouli that Peaveman associated with people of their type. It was more enigmatic. Alluring. Peaveman cringed with urgency. He needed to sort out if this person was under-aged, and some sort of tough girl or effeminate boy.

"You hulked out back there," the kid grinned at the top.

They reached down to help Peaveman manage the last painful step. "Was it super awesome?"

Clouds would have been nice. The sun on the roof was blinding. Peaveman refused the lift and squinted at the kid. "I don't know."

"It looked so awesome. Did it feel like, you know, *Raawr*!" The kid made a weak giggling sound after the animal imitation and shook two slender fists in the air. The nails were not short. Not painted. The giggle was like a fresh jet of water.

The kid's magnetic joy splashed on Peaveman. He swallowed his lukewarm saliva, unsure if his attraction called his masculinity into question. His throat hitched as if he was ready to cry. Instead of giving in to the sudden desire to throw his arms around the kid and bury his face in every cleft, he stood up straight like a good soldier and said, "There was no other way. It had to be done."

The existence of the snack machine made Peaveman depressed under normal circumstances. Witnessing the contents dwindle and then remain irrevocably depleted with no hope of re-supply was too much pain to bear. Not only was the fake food bereft of nutrition and void of any flavor. The mass-marketed chemical-additive-laced products designed to perpetuate an addictive, momentary gratification were almost all gone. The loss of what was barely adequate to begin with was intolerable.

Peaveman said, "I had to take a stand. Guess I lost my job."

"Don't worry about that. They'll never know it's you."

Reassurance that he would not escape employment was worse than the thought of being fired. Peaveman protested. "They'll know. They'll see that I never came back from my break."

"Half the people hired don't come back from their breaks. Like, you know, ever." The kid giggled again and Peaveman censored the wish to dive at them and wrestle the kid into torrents of erotic laughter, rolling around on the rooftop, ignoring the rocks, broken glass, and bird shit. If only he could see the kid better he'd feel less upset by his impulses.

"I always come back. They'll know."

Peaveman wasn't sure if he spoke from fatalism or

hope. He pictured write-ups in the news after his arrest. Some catchphrase akin to *going postal* might emerge as common slang, maybe *snack attack* or *candy crash* or *vendor avenger*. An outbreak of copycats destroying vending machines and snack bars and junk food dispensers all across the United States. Gumballs strewn across the highways, La Brea tar pits of dried soda trapping loud children inside schools and playgrounds, cereal aisles in grocery stores and quick marts doused in gasoline, storehouses of faux-nutrition going up in flames. Peaveman smiled at the thought.

"I'll cover for you," the kid said. "Be your alibi."

Peaveman tried to get a better look. Sunlight glinted off the many piercings. The glare made it impossible to gaze straight into the kid's face. If Peaveman stared too long, he saw a ring of fire encircling their head.

"How old are you? You didn't tell me your name."

"Hey, listen, I'll say I got sick and you gave me a lift home. They can't argue with helping me out. You have a car, right?"

"Not anymore. Wife took all that. I take the bus now." Peaveman rested his eyes and scanned the miniature streets twelve stories below. They crawled with toy cars and scurrying ant-people who carried tiny pheromone-laden briefcases that marked the trail towards success. He leaned over the ledge a little too far. "I think I hear sirens."

The kid leaned with him. "They won't search up here. You're safe with me."

"Until tomorrow or the next day. Then what?" Peaveman leaned further into the breeze and let the wind wrap his aching head in the kid's peculiarly soothing scent. Maybe masculinity didn't matter anymore. Maybe nothing did. Peaveman smiled at the kid tentatively and then dropped his eyes down to the street.

The ant farm activity had increased. Peaveman was glad to be above it for once. On the rooftop, he was outside of the glass looking in. The colorful creature next to him shimmered within reach. Without looking up again, he said: "At least jail will be a change. I almost wish I'd done something worse."

The air shifted. The scent withdrew. Peaveman turned to make sure the kid was still there. The sirens below halted with a blip. Emergency flashers went out like dying fireflies in contrast to the kid's overwhelming brilliance. Peaveman tried to look. The kid blasted his eyes like the glare from a furnace.

They knelt and bowed. "Walk upon my sword."

Peaveman didn't see a sword, but he heard it. A chorus of light singing. Bright air whistling in his ears.

"Why me?"

The kid's clear voice rolled across the rooftop like a cool wind. "I won't let them take you from me."

"Shit, I need a girlfriend, not a guardian angel." Peaveman shielded his eyes and tried to glimpse the kid, holding his hands like a visor. "What are you supposed to be?"

"Nothing," the kid said. "No one."

Peaveman's throat went dry and tight. "I need to go."

He turned. Tears smudged the corners of his eyes. He almost collided with a person standing right behind him. He edged sideways after the jolt. He didn't realize anyone else was up here. His elbow made contact with a fleshy midriff and his foot bumped a shoe on his other side. Peaveman recoiled. He was boxed in. People were everywhere. They lurked between the carbines and rooftop vents. They huddled under the shallow awnings of equipment casings. They stood in piles of debris and pigeon dung, crowded in a dumb mass under the sun. They faced Peaveman in silence.

As if he were a monster cornered by an accusing mob, Peaveman braced to make his villain's proclamation. *Here I am, you cowards, you sheep. You found me. You'll thank me when you wake up out of your stupor! There's nothing! Nothing!*

His voice caught when he noticed the blood spattered on their clothes. The snack machine must have flung shrapnel on impact and caused an outrageous number of injuries. Stuttering with guilt, Peaveman tried to apologize to a young woman nearby. Her arm dangled in a very wrong manner. He couldn't get the words out. Below the bicep, her flesh was abraded and skinless. He thought he saw a sliver of bone. Peaveman cried out in disgust and remorse.

He cowered. The mob surrounded him. Not one person

remained unharmed.

Peaveman's eyes flew in every direction seeking escape. Everywhere he looked, dislocated shoulders, shattered knees. Splintered skulls leaking chunky, liquefied contents erupting from half a face. Between the wounded who stood upright, Peaveman glimpsed dismembered suggestions of prone victims. Too twisted to stand, their limbs floundered like bad acrobats. Some were little more than crimson puddles of hands, hair, and meat. Peaveman swung around and shrank from the throng.

"No, I'm sorry, I can't—it wasn't me." Peaveman found his voice. But he had no defense. He was the coward. He was the sheep. He put his face in his hands, closed his eyes, and wept.

It couldn't be true. He'd seen the snack machine fall. The empty stairwell was clear before it dropped. The doors on each floor had automatic closures according to fire safety regulations. They swung in toward the stairwell. He didn't understand how they'd blast open from the snack machine's impact.

He cried into his guilty hands. "What do you want from me?"

The throng didn't answer.

Peaveman raised his remorseful face. One exploding snack machine had crushed and mangled this vast mob ready to swarm him.

But they didn't swarm. They hovered, close yet indifferent.

Like all the people in Peaveman's life.

He was used to it. He was sick of it. He was sick of being used to it.

He screamed. His voice cracked. "Okay, I did it. Come and get me you assholes. Do your worst!"

Nothing happened.

Peaveman shoved. The bodies swayed like heavy carcasses and came back to rest. They formed an impenetrable wall of human meat. Pressed against the ledge, Peaveman begged the kneeling kid for help.

"Get them away from me. Get me out of here. What's happening?"

"Come forward," the kid said. "And tread upon my

sword." No longer invisible, the sword stretched across the gravel rooftop floor. Peaveman heard it singing, saw it glimmering.

The kid was now unbearable to behold, made of light, silver, steel, and jewels. Peaveman suspected a siren sent to lure him to doom; yet the sword sang his name with singular knowledge. The indifferent mob that crowded him off the rooftop was no different than the crowds that railroaded him out of his life and out of his love and into doom as he'd known it too often. Through the disappointment of others, through guilt, through loss, through litigation, the kid's image burned brighter than a star. Peaveman defied his anonymous annihilation and grabbed the hilt of an intimate damnation he hoped to call his very own.

He stepped onto the sword. Pain shot through his body. The blade swung over the ledge. Peaveman balanced in midair. He gasped in fear. The kid blinded him with fire. Now molten inside, his agony turned into bliss. It slid through him and out of him, soaking the sword. In one gesture, the kid lifted the sword, cleaved Peaveman in half and clad him in gold. They both fell.

As the sword sliced through the air, the kid stripped. Peaveman knew them and needed them without indifference or sorrow. The kid bucked and clawed. With the many arms of a spider, the kid spun Peaveman into a sarcophagus that held the undisclosed riches of a feral identity. Concentrated inside his casing, Peaveman liquefied and supplied hot magma to his host.

Falling was not flying. The sidewalk grit of the commercial district rushed at Peaveman's skull. Encased in gold as the city herself was encased in concrete, Peaveman acknowledged the consequences of falling. "What will happen when we meet again?"

The voice of the kid answered with a tittering giggle afterward. "Then you will know us, and through us, you will also be revealed."

The fall was fast. Stillness held the center. Heavier by the second, gold and glitter glorified Peaveman's pulse. Liquid in rushing air, no way out, no chance to flee, to plead for life, falling, falling without reprieve, falling. Peaveman froze.

The molten gold inside Peaveman hardened into brittle mesh. The kid gripped him with all their arms before the bones collapsed. They clenched the tense sensation of Peaveman's petrified organs. The kid pulled out the soft parts and left a quivering shell like a water balloon. Peaveman's panic burst upon impact. The kid savored this part, drank it in like an endless diet grape soda and crushed the empty can when it was drained.

Peaveman met the ground upside down in a decapitating crunch.

In the moment between brain death and the crack of his neck, before Peaveman's aural imprint joined the kid's collection in the skyscraper's hungry rooftop maw, after Peaveman's cervical vertebrae ripped apart and his carotid arteries popped; in that brief pause when Peaveman's body stopped and his severed head bounded with autonomous joy on a trajectory of total freedom; for that instant, Peaveman lamented that his richest intimacy had been in falling, and that as his head hit the street for the third time, he knew the gold hidden within him would shatter and forever be lost.

Swanmord

King Hera slaps the ground and another zoo sutures through the concrete. Her eyes don't open. Her facial flesh puckers. Lids rot closed, slits under dung of swans placed there as a poultice. Healed, her eyes implode. New museums birth atrocity in every flex. Her sword flags. Her codpiece wags. Blooming like candy, king mother Hera births the next exhibit due to populate the bestiary: clove, astringent, and amaranth. Corporeal, she sings a son towards a swan dive. Hayden takes two pills from his stash and confirms sufficient inventory to unmother an existence blooded on protest. With appropriate doses, he'll make it through the night before smashing the whole damn archive.

In a tenor too high to persuade, Hayden serenades Trillious. "I am the DJ, I am what I play." He traverses the room on tip-toes, teetering on invisible high heels. At the foot of the bed he poses, watching Trillious frown and sketch. "Feel free to remain and admire my body as long as you like." Hayden twists at the hips like a glamorous tightrope walker, first left, then right, thickly, imitating heavier wedges. "Shall I lie upon the bed and adopt a languid demeanor for you, darling?"

Poor Trillious, downgraded to one night stand programmed on repeat, shakes their head without ceasing to sketch. "I'm drawing a tarot deck of all my lovers. You're the King of Toilets. Don't change a thing."

"I want to be your toilet. Let's wrap our tongues around

each other."

"You can never stop fidgeting long enough for that level of adult commitment. I don't know why you asked me here again just to insist on making fun of me and mocking my very serious art."

Hayden wants to answer with a fart, but he's striving to maintain the illusion that he's not a twelve-year-old boy beneath his manly body. It is manly, isn't it? Though slender and shaky as a baby bird's leg from his neck to his groin, arms long and white as a swan's throat, it's fundamentally flat in the right places and bulges nicely at the biceps when he wears the right jacket. His father blessed him with a square jaw and a love of good craftsmanship that shows in his careful construction of persona. His mother cursed him with deific genes and a moody heart.

"One of these days, if I'm lucky, I'll learn what it's like to feel the tip of a sharp beak when it enters like a needle and pries the red flaps between my ventricles apart," he says. Hayden hates mother Hera for letting him slip through one of her open wounds with the manifold ease of a hydra in heat. He wishes he'd been man enough as an infant to cause fatal harm in his immortal descent. "You'll never understand. I was born to be adored, a king amongst toilets. A swan amongst songbirds. A muted ace."

Trillious glares at the sketchpad, dissatisfied. "It's always the wrong people who die, isn't it?"

Hayden imagines himself a hysterical hydra, choking with multiple throats. Multiple deaths elude him. Lips pouting, accentuating leftover impressions of acne that pit the edges of his chin and cheeks: "Are you dreaming of my immaculate skin?" Above his wide eyes, forehead scars grow more visible as his hair recedes. Imperfections he embraces, evidence of a body at war. Covered in the skin of Hera's discarded shields, Hayden hopes an ancient leather garment will supplant his youthful glow with battle scars.

Swift corruption is all he can hope for as an idol. Like his dad said, everyone on the scene aged ten years overnight when Ian Curtis died. Music changed. "No balls," his dad summed up in an accent heavy with forbidden elixirs. Secrets upon secrets in the blended cadmium hues. Hayden sneers at his handsome reflection as it wavers from turpentine fumes in the dresser mirror. Ian Curtis shakes pinned on the wall nearby, ecstatic eyes rolled back to whites, a St. Vitus dance beside Hayden's effeminate prance. The slick poster paper cracks with a history of humidity in the vintage fibers. Hayden's dad left him enough money to do something about it. He could get its conservation- framed, but that's a sacrilege against the memorial of an honest death that Hayden's not willing to broach.

Death of aesthetics, or monstrous birth? Hayden's birthday is today, May eighteenth. His dad shrugged about the coincidence with closed lips and a knowing look. Their inside joke, though neither one laughed. Hayden kept quiet around his father and listened hard. Sorting evidence from disdain was no simple child's task. It's no surprise *Closer* was the first vinyl Hayden bought with his babysitting money when he was a blushing schoolgirl. Even now it's his go-to album for intoxicated anal sex.

"The suit of toilets encompasses the elements of porcelain and shit." Trillious makes corrections to their drawing. Smudges with a pinky and cocks their head. Gentle frown lines accent the lack of irony. "Contrast informs the proposed deck. The card suits are uncountable: porcelain, attention, dogma, and clarity. In the absence of numeration, the diminutive cards following trumps and royals bear fidelity or opposition to their theme to communicate both rank and import. The Ace is ever-changing, and far from mute. It alters the reading based on whether the interpreter calls it a one or a zero."

"Darling, you said there aren't any numbers. You'll make a terrible witness when they charge you for my crimes. Of course I plan to frame you when I hang." Hayden jabs his tongue out of the side of his mouth in mock strangulation.

Trillious is unmoved. "Numbers exist, with or without the formality of counting. In my deck, suits may appropriate cards from other suits, lending fluidity to divination that some users find vexing. I refuse to corrupt my design. Its ambiguous leanings make it rich in possibility and lore."

They turn the sketchbook to display Hayden's graven

image. Frown lines blur into a sly smile over the metal coil connecting pages across the top. One side of the wire is bent at a dangerous angle, its convoluted end unraveled and sharp. Trillious's tone shares a similar path. "I expect to encounter resistance to confusion and uncertainty. It seems no one wants their oracles to be too damn lifelike."

Conscious of the eyes ogling his handsome body, Hayden shifts the cage of skin containing the raw meat of nothingness that feeds the sharks of time inside him. In contrast to the stillness of desire, Hayden yells, twitching. "Well, you certainly can't accuse me of that!"

Always, he feels desire. He twitches faster, growing violent, jerking his shoulders, his knees, and tossing his head atop a cracking neck. He empties out his needs fearfully, like a sea cucumber. Open and erupting, Hayden's a disgorged vessel. A solid lack. Collapsing on the bed, his vocalizations turn asemic.

Trillious tackles Hayden. The sketchpad drops. The page is crushed. Hayden's iconic image mimics his fit. Trillious tries to restrain him and defer the damage of his epileptic dance. Spurious or sincere, a history of black eyes, bruises, and lumps litters the subcutaneous fascia of any fan foolish enough to fall prey to Hayden's drama.

He wrenches away from Trillious. They swing wide over his legs and renew their grip.

Hayden's deep enough in the archive to know this candy wrapper's going straight in the trash the minute he rips it off. Knees slap tender flesh-upholstered bone. Hera slaps the ground and births a new conundrum. Hayden's one of many, monstered out of borrowed parts and bitter vengeance. Excited by his lover's participatory indulgence, he really needs to figure out if this drama has a tragic or comedic arc before they get too close to the ending. Struggling against Trillious, reveling in illness, Hayden garbles out chunks of his unceasing inner monologue. "How dare you claim to care? Pantheon addict. As if I'm your gateway drug to corrupted kings. Drama is my derelict birthright, by all the gods before me."

Pressed on top of Hayden, Trillious giggles, thighs and

belly like a sarcophagus full of baked beans, shifting. "But I'm your biggest fan."

"Rotten, rotten; I smell of kings. Kill them all. Kiss off."

"Kiss all kings," and Trillious tries to catch his lips.

Hayden bucks against hips fleshed hysterical as Hera's. He's hard with hate at their wide expanse and forgiving angles, at the loneliness they breed promising all the wrong kinds of pain for a masochist his age. Hayden's worked long and hard to be long and hard. He eschews softness.

Unbalancing his opponent by locking a shin beneath their knee, Hayden grasps their waist and shoulder and pins Trillious on the bed. Hayden's on top, trumpeting desire. "You can't possibly expect me to keep my hands off your throat in this torrid Greek climate, you silly cocksucker."

Hayden tears away lacy packaging and pearls, exposing a creature like a baby rhinoceros that nudges his cunt. Blind with mammalian greed, it seeks a gland to suckle upon. The wrestlers' mutual laughter escalates into breathless screams. Hayden's elbow punctures the portrait. His flying spittle pockmarks the crumpled sketch.

"I can't stand these terrible panties." Hayden intends to roar. Instead, he emits a febrile whine that's followed too soon by gushing tears. "How much do you think I can take? I can't handle any of this situation with you. You taste like imported textiles, all musty. Shitty panties like a grandmother, these bouncing clown ears, deceptive frills. Your majestic confluence with ocular anomalies cracks my skull."

The creature between them grunts. Hayden strangles Trillious's bulging throat. "The window dressing you hang on my life, when I'm the thing hanging, I'm what should be hung. I mean hanged. For fuck's sake, I can't even get the past tense of my own suicide correct. No wonder you hate me. You're all I have. I can't live without you. It's disgusting. I've lost control. I'm a fat old hen sewn into a sack of rocks, unable to drown. My god, look at your hideous face."

Trillious gargles. A snakelike tongue protrudes from puffy lips. Foam the color of weak tea gathers. Hayden tastes it, wincing at the smoky rottenness of his recently ingested stench. He sucks hard on the sore tongue and plunges his free hand into Trillious, prodding desperately, hopelessly, pausing long enough to swallow the cascade of moans released from their neck. Hayden shudders. Trillious lies slack as an old shirt.

Pulling out, Hayden tosses away the shredded fabric he detests. Bright red fingerprints adorn Trillious. Their Adam's apple churns like a conqueror worm. Hayden wipes their face with the back of his fist, smearing more than he cleans.

‡

Pausing with wet knuckles pressed into a soft cheek. "Nothing's real about you. Not your sacrificial panties, or your squirming malachite disguise. You've been a right scheming bitch from the start. You make a satire of love." Jack of all jacks, Hayden's satisfied and disgusted with the mess he's made of Trillious. He's ready to accept his punishment.

He's dying for it.

Reclining in gasps, Trillious coughs out a croak that smooths into husky grunge. "Satyr of love, sinner of all sins, heretic of all heretics. You'll form a hybrid beast of us in ample time. I love you. How I love you. Ribs growing through our skulls like antlers, antlers peeling like cinnamon bark, barking swans swallowing their infinite tails. Feathers of men."

Hayden shakes at the thought of unbridled connection and mutation. "God, can't you just hit me like a normal behemoth?"

His weight evaporates. He digs through the dresser drawer to pilfer his stash for an anchor. He can't stop thinking about someone cutting off his legs and replacing them with overripe carrots. Left a screaming mandrake, sutured back into the earth from which he was torn to embody Hera's revenge, he'd be responsible for more massacres than his current budget allows.

The wall shakes, Ian Curtis always dancing, if anyone still calls it that, marking elaborate time signatures Hayden wants to recreate in his next set. The sensitive man on the poster barely hides the mobled queen beneath. Hayden hears her rustling under the surface of things, threatening to sleepwalk all over his fragile libido. Evidence stains his sheets. Mother Hera haunts the walls, stapled like the plastic barricading a crime scene. Hayden's hardest job is holding her flat.

"Are you okay? That last dose was enough to abort an albatross."

"One of us needs the steel to die like a madman instead of merely dipping our necks in the sludge for a snack. If you hack it off," Hayden says, "let me have it. I see you looking good in taxidermy for the archive. We can start fresh with a new wing."

Palms brushing away strained tears, bile squeezed from an enamored head, Trillious sighs in adulation. "I'm your biggest fan. Trust me, this isn't about him. It never was. I worship you. There's nothing you can do to make me stop loving you, no matter how rotten you pretend to get. Why do you insist on staying in this hole year after year? Let's grow new tails and learn to swim. Let's leave history behind us."

The cracks in the archive are spreading. The walls are as weak as shocked granite, unsuitable for either construction development or common culinary use. A web of flaws unravels the cognitive structures Hayden holds dear. Bare sustenance splayed open in the spider web of cracks, he feels the opposite of a fly, struggling to stay trapped.

Trillious is transformation, stalking him in the tenement halls long before the archive fell out of some demiurge's asshole and landed on earth. They started out young and sneaky, offering to do odd jobs. First it was cheap, then it was free. Somewhere along the way, the sketch pad manifested, Trillious fawning over Hayden's young drunken grace. Drunk on cough syrup in third grade, Hayden mourning his deific predilections. Trillious thrilled, proposed a trade. The attention neutered Hayden for days, but of course he sat for the portraits. Of course he agreed.

Careless beauty sloughs off onto the page. Hayden's old skins pinned to the wall have a bad habit of growing nipples. Pores inflate with glandular excess. Trillious tacks up terrible reminders of what screams beneath Hayden's skin. When the windows are open, Hayden and Hera dance a fluttering paper duet on the walls.

Hayden gulps three tablets dry. Two for expulsion and one for pain. "The king of toilets is working up to one flaming crescendo. I'd birth it in your mouth if I didn't suspect you'd enjoy the experience so much."

"There are infinite ways to fill and be filled."

"I don't want to spoil you, darling. Not just yet. Turn around. Bend over. Don't look at me."

Trillious obeys. "How precious our offspring will be before they drown in menstrual blood, my love. How intrinsically divine. Your perfect jawline, my malachite eyes, and a triton for a tail."

Hayden's angle of approach reveals Trillious gloating with a murderer's possessive gaze. Their images mate in the mirror like rival songbirds. Hayden's hips flex in parallel aggression with each gluteal thrust. Trillious is bent into a scaffold of indecency, emitting the cyan enzyme of an unwilling slave to biology.

Lilting like a chariot pulled by peacocks, Trillious lectures. "The respective elements of the four suits are air, fire, earth and water." They brush their hairless arms against Hayden's heaving chest, turning tail feathers with gemstone eyes on his motions. "Clarity as water is mutable, evoking its opposite: confusion. You know about that. The duality of the fourth suit creates a fifth ghost suit, if you will. There are no cards for the ghost suit. It is, however, the most important of all five with the corresponding element of ether." Trillious gasps as Hayden heaves into them. "I'm serious. What I mean by all this is that we can be happy together. I've never feared your rages, your moods."

Fascinated by his own transparent skin, Hayden eradicates eye contact. "Isn't there somewhere else you need to be?"

"Are you listening?"

"Don't whine, darling," Hayden says.

How he remains opaque to anyone else is unfathomable. Through his frail tissue paper of epidermis, Hayden watches the writhing black coils of putrefaction that compose his insides. Some are large and thick like rubber hoses, others small and delicate as string. Maggots dance like dollops of static. Multiple roots of abscesses weave a lugubrious pattern of linear uncertainty. The footwork for his partners to follow is complicated and variable. Who Hayden becomes from one day to the next is up for grabs.

A body rots inside him. What a sham, this eternal shifting skin.

Hayden gluts on black market misoprostol and fentanyl.

Another dose, another monstrous birth averted.

‡

Hayden isn't sure why he's so cold or why fucking seems fucking impossible these days. Trillious's voice is indistinct over the loud music and the clamor of the crowd of dance-crazed skins erupting from the walls. Hayden places vinyl on the turntable, fits the needle to the initiatory groove and fades up. From one son to the next, no, he meant to say from one *song* to the next, he considers the hopeful possibility that he's not on stage but actually overdosed and lying cold in bed while Trillious jerks his shoulders with the rhythm of a slam dance hoping he'll revive.

Another day, another suicide. Hayden stains the archive with redundant attempts. The safe spaces he sticks with imprint image after image of crippled gods erupting from concrete. King Hera limps in Hayden's footsteps, following his faun-like outline. Hayden stays one pivot ahead, one kick past parental censure, one stage dive closer to zooicide.

The violence of the dance snaps his head to and fro. When Hayden's neck lolls back, he almost chokes. Trillious tenderly coaxes his face upright next. Holds Hayden's forehead close to their lips. Whispers. "I worship you. I'm your biggest fan."

"Oh god, that's not creepy at all," Hayden says, but no sound comes out.

For his next set, Hayden has no idea what kind of musical theme to disseminate. Fortunately, the intimate whispering transfers to the speakers, Trillious crosses the dancefloor, and the song doesn't stop. Hayden can't figure out why there's a bed on stage. If he had any energy he'd tell the owner to cut the strobe, too. His retinas throb in syncopated time with the cycles of the turntable and the flashing lights.

Trillious brings him a drink, slinking to the beat and yelling soundlessly across an extended cup. Hayden tastes it and spits. "What the fuck?"

"Everything goes better with hemlock, my love."

Hayden downs the drink in one gulp. "Prove it. The extension of mercy. The dour fountain staunched."

The dim apartment, the bed, the archive: it all flips like a costume change. Every skin on the wall breathes, an outfit wide awake, waiting for a lover to wear it and become fully fleshed. Creatures craving the gift of life. Unwilling idol, hell-bent on sacrifice, Hayden clasps Trillious through the fog of his fast panic gasps. Crushed by the embrace, Trillious murmurs with dry lips into Hayden's straining chest where the stubborn heart of a half-god flutters. "That's more than I could hope for." Trillious presses their face in the softness to the side of Hayden's sternum. "I'm not trying to be ironic. You must know pregnancy increases the risk of thrombosis."

Hayden's unable to draw enough sustenance into his lungs to get more than a word out: "Finish."

Trillious yanks Hayden's belt. It takes extra effort to loosen the clasp with all the weight Hayden's put on. Trillious pulls. The belt slides free like a snake. Trillious drops it on the floor and releases Hayden's gut from his trousers. "It's a question of verisimilitude. How much are you really willing to commit to being plausible? How willing are you to nibble the obscure marrow?"

Hayden's belly swells into a gigantic mound as it slathers out of his fly. "I prefer to wallow in aspiration, lapping at sightless passages." He hiccups. "Oh god, I'm going to be sick."

Carpet smells of unwashed feet mix with dust-clumped desires. The mold growing beneath the surface in the damp foam pad flattens under Hayden's gravid weight. Running and retching, Hayden streams bile across the worn former plush. He slumps shy of the toilet. The mound in his gut kicks. Each hit cracks Hayden's breath into painful splinters.

Codpiece in clown panties, lips like Hera's, pursed, Trillious has grown too massive to fit through the bathroom door.

They bellow in a corrugated slur, thickened like chins. "We're eating for two now. No coddling your precious beauty. I've made a fresh portrait of you."

Nurse Trillious extends a new limb which is not an arm or a branch or a corkscrew-shaped duck penis that spins with the arrhythmia of St. Vitus dance. It pierces Hayden's belly, shuddering and splattering a new hole. Galvanized, Hayden's spit flows like a river of egg white. The taste of sickness slides freely between his jaws. His guts are slam dancing. Babies bruise tender spleen and cartilage within him. His tumors have finally turned on him, perforating the elastic reproductive organ he thought atrophied. Hayden's abortions fight for an exit wound, devouring their disposable host on the trip down the death canal.

Each turn of the screw brings him closer to sweet release.

Villi escape like errant intentions, paving the way to heavenly unconsciousness. Warm liquids flood Hayden's vast cavity. His reward is within reach. Holy Hera, king of cunts, Trillious nurses a lathered tip into Hayden's mangled slit. In response, Hayden squeezes their prickly skin, milking analgesic pus from engorged pores. The stitches in archival rag barely hold. The nurse costume slips. Breasts between men seek a new bearer. Tissue samples flee below foreign skin.

Once again congealed in blubbery chaos, Trillious punches Hayden in the stomach. "I'm your biggest fan." Their voice doubles in the echoing emptiness of Hayden's abdomen. "I will make my home in you, where your father lies."

The nauseous pain of the gut punch sends Hayden into an aphrodisiac head spin. Revolving waves overcome his resistance. He's blinking in and out, each glimpse of light an overwhelming and unwelcome ping of pleasure.

Trillious drilling: "Jack of all jacks. I'll grant you an exegesis in red."

Describe the vinyl. Needle skips through blackened grooves. Impressions scratch away all cogent sound. Trillious squeezes the satyr to death in the eyeless channel of an overgrown lock. Hayden's orgasm stops when he finds his father shot.

‡

Here his father lies. The blood-pool is sticky where time darkens the liquid, no longer flowing. How long he lay in the apartment alone is a matter for medical examiners to sort. No weapon is located onsite. The bullet pattern indicates an amateur, ruling out a professional hit, although it's everyone's first thought. The rich artist's ties to a certain underworld boss were common lore. They came up in the worker's union together, parted ways in the eighties. Hayden's dad claimed no contact, reports of involvement persisted, part of the man's illustrious mystique. With a cushion of prosperity against serious inquiries, the master craftsman turned master publicist and made the most of notorious rumors.

Hayden wished him dead, of course. The old man was cruel to his untalented mongrel progeny, disdained the proof and product of deific deception. King Hera, Queen of Heaven, meting out her twisted justice of fecundity. She slaps the ground and vomits up a hairball that grows into a bountiful apple orchard. She kicks a brick foundation and the church upon it leaks a pheromone elixir that causes the congregation to ovulate. She grabs a swan by the throat and it farts out a luxuriously endowed trio of dwarves whose laughter impregnates nearby cattle. Suffering from dementia for eons, her doddering fertility rites welcome abusive suitors. Hayden's dad was one fool of many.

But wishes are lies.

When Hayden finds his father shot, the restless bulk of the unmoving masculine body alerts his senses before he sees any blood. The position is all wrong. Lumped over an arm, v-shaped neck thrust back, the garrulous mouth sprouts a slack tongue. Hayden wonders why his socks are wet. He doesn't register how they've soaked up the dead man's blood because he's stood there so long doing nothing.

Hayden can't move. He's trying to figure out why the noise didn't wake him. His room is right above the studio.

Dad lies calm as a bear carcass waiting for flies. Hayden bends and kneels, proving he's capable of moving. Wearing a pink nightgown and white ankle socks, he's baffled by the inordinate silence muffling every sound in the tenement. It's an old building where neighbors grow close like family. In the quiet, Hayden strains an arm over dad's corpulent waistline. His nine-year-old fingers fumble to undo his father's belt. He tries to overlook the modulated mouths of exit wounds and the sensation of a warm turd in the old man's pants. It molds to fit his knee. He yanks the last notch and the clasp comes free.

Hayden slides the belt through the loops and takes it into the kitchen. The water pipe is exposed across the ceiling. Hayden positions a chair beneath it. Still strangely deaf, he can't hear the chalkboard scraping of the legs scoring the floor. It's like being underwater. He hopes he won't float.

Looping the belt over the pipe is easy enough, but Hayden's long hair gets in the way of hanging. How he hates the old man for forbidding him to cut it. For making him wear skirts. How he hates himself for telling Trillious. Their grandmother kept a pearl-handled pistol hidden in the folds of her fat flowered handbag in the suite next door.

The blushing schoolgirl hangs, growing beet red in the face. He watches the warm bear of his father's body growing cold in the corner of his eye. An immortal genepool denies Hayden mimicry of the man he admires.

An end to justice, an unsettling of debts. Silenced by slashes as drastic as the belt, Hayden takes refuge. In music. In corrugated silence. In archetypal lies. Nine or nine hundred years old, Hayden deviates into helpless rebellion. As Trillious guts him, Hayden realizes the master plan for his next set: three turntables, one dog.

Johnny Thunders live. Slumping, slurring, an intoxicated godhead. Message undermined. The variant is the position, the choice. Will you take the stage or feed it your wonder until the well runs dry? Sid Vicious next, with impossible vocals like a deprived child. Michael Gira wins with hopeless gravel drone metamorphosing into an altered verse: "And now I want to be your god."

Words of an idiot.

Slumping in undone innards on the bathroom floor.

Hanging from the kitchen water pipe overnight. Teaching a wound to speak. Too much time to contemplate Hera's glory as a crust. She forms from his suicides, matron dissected in reverse. Wallpaper tears where the nine-year-old hangs without hanging, chokes without choking. Strangled into silence, the child helpless as Hera peels flesh long trapped in battlements and fills up her lumpy form. She steps, unsteady, ripping out doll stitches, sword lowered, poised for havoc, for gutting guilty swans, for plucking pearls from a murderer's eyes. Fragile in strength, the blind goddess wobbles as much as she kills.

"Uh, secular," Hayden moans. The warning is explicitly missed.

‡

Hayden cries.

"I'm dreaming, I'm dying, this is an overdose. I'm hallucinating my next suicide. This can't be real, it can't." But it is real. As real as Trillious ripping into Hayden's unwanted organ, thus solving the problem of its unwanted contents.

Hayden hating, emptied of erotic inhabitants with his womanhood spread. It spins Hayden's head. Like a record baby right round. His wound whispers and weeps with the beat. Thighs tensed, back arched, ass flexed, Hayden's hollows howl.

Trillious quenching their thirst for impalement and repetition. "I'll do anything for you."

Distended and retracted in wet flaps, Hayden's begging for the kid to see King Hera hulking behind them. Taking in their sounds and returning his own, he's dreaming of a fiendish diagnostic idol, of asylum with a hemlock-cured misanthrope, buzz buzz into the secular modification connector. "I'm worthless," Hayden groans.

Trillious says, "Try to be more careful. Next time you're going to hemorrhage or get an infection."

"I hate you."

"I worship you."

"Don't leave me. How could you leave me?"

Guilty as a swan, Hayden hides trembling in the archive as King Hera descends, clavicles cocked. She of the ready sword and imploded eyes, she of the suckling ragged skins and shredded clown disguise, she of memory loss and staggering idiot vengeance. She, King Hera, Spring Virgin, Summer Mother, Autumn Crone, Winter King, totters from Olympus to fuck another swan and be fucked. The mythic circle of immortal life, the fallacy of return, and the corruption of sickly gods. Hayden sees her face in the mirror behind Trillious.

Bound downward, ancient harridan King Hera slaps the ground and births an infinite number of roaring reiterations of her husk, her cunt, her mane. Gathered and tethered, Trillious falling prey, pickling into a permanent girl, joining the shriveled imitations lining the archive, lost dolls and mutated suitors, fans and foes trapped within King Hera's skin.

Hayden can't stand it. Not again.

Mother Hera mocks Hayden's desire with Trillious limp in her grip. This time, Hayden doesn't turn away. He shoves his unrenewed virginity between captor and slave. Trillious is freed from Hera's all-consuming stitches in a tumble of bull skulls and cuckoo feathers. Parts of Hayden sloughed off in passion leave him like ready traitors. The unwholesome effort overthrows his magical biology. Trillious loses sight of the collapsed idol bleeding out on the crowded dance floor. Their offspring scatter.

Hayden faces Hera alone. For a moment he feels more like a real man than ever. With toxic castration, with quivering archive, with dreams of defeat, with carnivorous bravado, with monstrous birth from monstrous birth, with monstrous birth from monstrous loins, he screams at Trillious, and Hera's nipples wither. "I am what I devour, I am what I own, love me, admire me, I hate you, you cocksucker. I can't live without you. Don't leave me. I love you. I've lost control."

MR. BONES
PUZZLE CANDY

The hothouse arousal of the undertaker's hand hit her like a wet brick, a slab covered in slip. She squeezed his fingers like clay digits that begged to be molded for the kiln's curing fire. Her tips rubbed his knuckles, and the puzzle of his bones assembled in her palm. He was a slim man.

One handshake, and her husband intervened, weight crushing wonder. It was his grandmother, after all. She attested his choices in silence. He labored to justify the cheapest urn while the undertaker offered reassurance. When the thin man caught her eye as quick as a hummingbird, she turned away.

It wasn't her husband's age. Twelve years wasn't that much. The shape of the marriage ground her raw. Sex dampened at odd angles, more rigor than pleasure. Where once her curves filled his sheer slope of muscle and bone, now his budding gut pushed her away. His altered diet moved his lumps to strange places. She cringed when he tasted wrong, evaded his sticky tongue and tainted breath. The musty smell of recent steak caught in the back of her throat. She saw heart attacks in the marbled meat he slapped in a pan, felt her gullet rise every time she came home to the sheen and smell of splattered grease.

She had a sweet tooth. Preferred buzz over bulk.

The sting of spun sugar, hummingbird bones full of air. The undertaker's bones hummed to her.

The night before the service, her husband slathered her

in grease, an engine of meat bloated with unspoken grief. She turned over when he was done. *Stick a fork in me, a knife, a scythe,* she thought, and thin fingers like lurid bones probed her to sleep.

Overtaken by the undertaker in erotic dreams, by sunken cheeks and taut forehead, saran-wrapped skin clinging to a skeletal structure ready to break free through the surface of sallow flesh, she felt his many-jointed fingers in her folds. The undertaker's touch was specific, knowing, and inarguable. She didn't need to be filled with fat. Segmented bones lodged and vibrated in all her pleasure points.

Grooming for the funeral like dressing for a date. Shame at her itch and impatience, awkward as a stranger through the service, endless stories of a past she didn't share. She grew more restless and abashed each time they called her *the new wife*.

Too many cocktails later, she disappeared into the funeral parlor to find him. Was it so wrong to flirt? She crept past the cloakroom and imagined long fingers pulling her down between the coats, fingers that handled the dead freezing her skin with forbidden knowledge. Airy gaps between his bones left her breathless; sharp pelvis jabbed with every slam of his hips.

The rustle of coats, heavy, woolen, black. Curtains dividing dreams. Forest of fabric shifting into darkness, as if the room went on forever.

The sensation of a needle stung the back of her neck.

She clasped her nape and turned. Bones baring sunken eyes, slim fitted suit draping loose, smile quietly manic. He put his finger against her lips. His other hand circled her waist and waltzed her backwards into the deep closet.

Shapes of coats, a crowd gathered in anonymous black, rustling; heavy men hanging by their necks. Colder as she backed through the recesses, not coats but carcasses hanging and swinging. Dead men blackened with rot, rustle of vermin under coats of flesh. The points of the undertaker's fingers inspecting her body for arousal. Waltzing, wet under her dress, back pressed against something warm, the undertaker slipping his fingers in and out and holding up his hand to show her the bare bones.

His skin was stripped, muscle and nerve eaten away. Warm

carcasses swung as the room rotated. Once again he placed a bone to her lips. She smelled the sugar in it, felt the squirm of something fragrant in the rotting meat, the slab behind her back alive and moist, massaging her with maggots.

The undertaker teased her mouth with a slim digit. "You know you want it."

She did.

She bit off the finger and crunched through the bone. Sugar stung the joints in her jaw. Sweetness hurt her back teeth. A hot tingle inflamed her cheeks. She reorganized the puzzle of his bones and ate all the candy, saving his manic grin for last. When his final tooth cracked open it heaved a cherry-flavored gasp.

She wiped the maggots from her back, flicked the ash from her dress, and grabbed her coat from the racks.

A heavy-set aunt blocked her exit. She resembled the husband if he were aged, fattened, and dressed in drag. "We've all been wondering where you ran off to."

Coat half on, half off. "I needed some air."

The matron looked her up and down. "I understand, dear. These things are so stressful."

Not budging, she plowed through her handbag and frowned into its depths over a double chin. The oversized tote didn't hide her excessive hips or opulent chest. She fished out a tissue, handed it to the wife, and tapped at the corner of her mouth.

"After you freshen up, come down to the tea room. I heard there's going to be cake."

The Revenge of Madeline Usher

What burns, what galls, what tortures is not his betrayal, but his theft. My love he owned from our earliest infant cries. He needed no fraud. My autonomy he acquired through means of the strange *malady* which the doctors he hired found final. Based on negligible evidence, the howl of a raw, impassioned tongue, the fire of a solitude unwilling to allow breach, the ricochet of moods most erratic and uncouth; with such scant proof as this—proof of a character *like his own* and known to me through private violence—my brother, Roderick, assumed legal ownership of my person and guardianship of my will.

Judge me not the sole mad Usher. Madness, a staple of our issue, runs wild in our men. The notoriety they enjoy as poets and masters of many arts surpasses all tangible creations. They make up in reputation what they lack in substance, and their genius achieves its greatest fruition in little more than the occasional ejaculation of an unproductive—albeit compelling—rant. Such was the fate of my brother. I tried to tame him. I tried to soothe him. I held him to my breast and took him in my mouth and still he chanted, still he raved—*Madman!–Do you not see?*

I held him in my mouth too oft, and the harsh liquor of madness soaked my throat. I loved him. I was a fool. What can I say? It was the only life I knew.

On the day before the stranger came, Roderick turned away from me in delicate agony. Delicately he bent down and sought my spoiled countenance. He pressed his thin lips into the stain of his own defilement. Forever piqued and unsated, he whispered a pledge to *hold* and *betroth*, exciting his fires anew. These fires feasted quickly upon their own flame and smoked as embers, scalding my sore lips. Perhaps I cringed.

"Demon!" he shrieked. "What more wilt thou take from me? My very soul?"

He shook me. His lips trembled like ribbons unraveled. His eyes burst from their sockets.

"No," I said. "I desire nothing."

The unnatural moisture of his eyes engorged and brightened them. They reeled like exploding planets. The musculature of his face quaked on the cusp of a maniac's laugh. And then, when the sound left him, it was the mirthless echo of dim remembered joys, the hollow cackle of the condemned.

He hovered. I knelt and held my frame as still as marble.

It was terror to breathe. One wrong sound, one ugly twitch, one incorrect gasp might send him careening into endless fury. Demon or sister or lover, I never knew which he summoned, which he shunned, which he held in amity or awe. The mystery of how I must behave at any given moment, of whence and how his cravings came and went and whether breathing itself broke his tryst or sealed it—all this seized and paralyzed my heart.

Though his reasons ever shifted, my quarantine remained constant. First, I was innocent, and must avoid the corruption of a world beyond my sweet understanding, remain a captive in our castle. Next, I was a devil, a concubine, a vein of poison snaking through the wholesome waters of God's good world: for the safety of all men, I must remain entombed within the walls of our ancestral home.

That I loved him, I have said. Love inextricably comingled with fear defined all our passions. We learned through the punishments meted out by our father. As children, as twins, Roderick and I trembled and suffered as one. Terror of our father's lash, his madness, his rheumy and accusing eyes—eyes bent upon revenge against his wife's infant murderers, for she had died soon after our birth—united us.

Behind the old man's back, we dared one another to mock our cruel oppressor. We reveled in perverse delights directly proportionate to the severity of our latest torture. With what thrilling deceit we plotted against him and pleasured our abused bodies! We vowed eternal fidelity and shared the scars of our castigation as emblems of our love.

Within the looming walls of our ancient home and the watery tarn that circled with humid embrace, I knew not that other mistresses walked free. No visitor or servant suggested I live otherwise; no cook or seamstress or scullery maid took me under her maternal wing. The women who passed through our walls under my father's employment regarded me with suspicion and dread as I walked hand in hand with my brother, and kissed his lips, and waited upon his every desire. To our father's violence and the visible results of his wrath, they played blind.

After the patriarch's blessed death, we were the last of our line. Roderick preserved our childhood solitude. What he hoped would unite us, drove us apart. I hid from his brutal attentions as I grew older and oft spied on him in his study. On one such melancholy day, the visitor came.

A man our age, perhaps twenty or twenty-five, with raven hair the tone Roderick bade me dye mine, and the pallid physique of a scholar. Roderick leapt from his sofa and burst into greeting. The guest returned his affection with moderate warmth. Roderick lapsed into silence, and the visitor gazed upon my brother with a look of *assessment* that I found chilling. I knew well the thickening of air between those who share secrets. My heart raced. Its heavy, horrible beating was so loud I feared it might betray my hiding place.

The stranger waited upon Roderick. When my brother spoke, he plied his guest with tales of congenital madness, offered this as an excuse for years of neglect, and expressed a keen hope their boyhood fellowship might be revived. Plagued by my impending demise, Roderick suffered in dread and might himself perish if not distracted by his *dearest friend*. I listened with interest, for I knew not of our fatal diagnosis. I felt myself quite vibrant and wholesome in body and mind.

I leaned too close. The scholar spotted me, and I took flight. His eyes sparkled with dark amusement. He had heavy lashes and a soporific, pudgy face, but he was not too dull to catch a glimpse of my skirt as I fled round a corner. Further, he had wit enough to conceal my presence from the possessive gaze of his host.

Intimate with the passageways and particulars of our mansion, I returned as an invisible participant in the congress between Roderick and his raven-haired guest. I spied on them, and when the stranger was well engaged, I snuck into his chamber and took up his journal. If he wished his thoughts kept private, he should not have left the volume exposed on his nightstand advertising its gossip, for he had witnessed my mobility and health!

He rudely disparaged our estate and family, painting a scene from Fuseli where our mansion and mental health decayed. He admitted a letter from Roderick had beckoned him and claimed the impassioned plea quite puzzling. Roderick, little more than an acquaintance, had been purged from his thoughts since boyhood. Yet I sensed deception: to this distant classmate of little importance and less love, the stranger had rushed without delay.

Roderick's devotion to his guest created—or perhaps recreated—an *acclimation* to close physical camaraderie. Flights of mood and the interplay of Roderick's manic and morose treatments tangled anxiety with ecstasy. Wild nights of song uplifted the pair to the apex of exaltation; in the next breath, Roderick's misery drained all joy and scoured the depths of hell. The stranger *adjusted* his moods to suit his host. What he once offered for reassurance as a hearty clap on the back now lingered in time and proximity much like an embrace.

I recognized Roderick's games of indoctrination and the fire in the guest's eyes—the building passion, frustration and gripping concern Roderick's behavior evoked, for I had borne my brother's seductions throughout my entire life.

I must warn him, I must flee. Both thoughts rang in my brain with rival urgency. The blaring of mental alarms deafened my reason and sickened my will. I chose to succumb to the illness assigned me and took to my bed. What words might pour forth if by accident or design, I confronted Roderick or exposed him to his guest?

Or shall I say it? Yes; yes, I must—his *victim*!

Roderick neglected my chamber. I raged with elation. I might celebrate with impunity, but oh the agony of guilt that gnawed into my brain! The stranger, the visitor—the poor wretch was my substitute!

An imp of anxiety chained my tongue. I must speak or flee. I did neither. The burden of speech sat upon my chest, a leering incubus that crushed my very breath. Never had I confessed to a stranger. Never had I dreamt of telling the sordid particulars of my story.

Uncertain of my course, I roused my frame and walked forth. I know not what inner angel guided my steps. My nerve failed when I spied the men on the divan in Roderick's library. Poetry and music culminated in hysterical laughter. The couple entwined with enervated exuberance and lay gazing like lovers. Roderick knew nothing of love, but he knew well how to wear love's mask and beguile the object of his lust. Laughter died. Roderick's eyes collapsed. His voice became thick with well-rehearsed pathos.

"Alas," he said. "The Lady Madeline is no more."

Did I dream? Did I somnambulate? Was I not conscious and lively as I learned news of my death?

The visitor's lips parted and closed and then parted again. He shook his head. Roderick trembled in the man's arms and then gave himself over to unspeakable howls of grief.

Through his moans, Roderick conveyed that in a black fit of sorrow he had sent all the servants away. He sobbed apology, for now, he said, the two of them were utterly and completely alone.

At this, the visitor took hold of Roderick with force. Although I had guessed my brother's intent, I failed to comprehend the full *corporeality* of what he desired and the unlikely attitudes it entailed. He who had so dominated my soul and ruled my body succumbed readily to the adept stranger's command.

My sanity hung in the balance at seeing my brother tamed. I questioned the veracity of my will and stumbled away, thoughts reeling. Why credit the ravings of a creature diagnosed with unnamed and incurable disease? Why hearken to she who appeared as immaterial as the dead in life's briefest glimpse, and lifelike in death once entombed? Why trust the voice of a ghost, a vampire, a victim? I knew not where to go or who to call upon. I had been void of agency for too long. I think I swooned, for after the revelation that my very thoughts were a twisted mirror I could no longer trust, my senses failed.

#

There is no peace in the grave. Tenuous hope pleaded for rescue or rest as the mourners attended me. Immobile, a fully aware cataleptic, I silently cried: *See me! I am alive! This body is a lie. Within this mute flesh, my mind is warm and vital! Release me*—I begged of the poison that percolated in my veins—*Release me and raise me, or have mercy, and by your quick potency end all thought!*

Roderick's guest and lover assisted with my internment and commented on the youthful charm of my lifelike blush.

Yes! But not lifelike, not "like"–for I am truly alive!

The paralysis of false death maintained its chill grasp on my stagnant muscles and leaden tongue. Dread fondled me with cold fingers as Roderick tucked my unresponsive limbs beneath the silken linings of the prepared box. Before the lid closed, his disingenuous teardrop teased, its splash upon my eye too gentle to revive, too buoyant to spur a blink.

I screamed. No sound came out. My jaw did not flex, my throat did not grind. My limp tongue lay imprisoned behind a peaceful smirk. My body was a puppet with no master. In my mind I screamed and pounded and threw off the cool silk of the clinging shroud; I shrieked and tore at the heavy lid. But in truth, my body was a useless doll posed to mimic peace.

In the twilight of the closed coffin, I was lifted, rocked and jolted. Rough handling failed to shatter the spell. Twilight turned to midnight and the hammering of nails snuffed out the dying light. Receding footsteps left me wide-eyed inside a black and inescapable cave.

There is no peace in the grave. Rest came not to my living corpse, for a noisome banquet began once my presence was scented. All manner of subterranean life tested the meat of my vulnerable flesh. Nibbling mandibles and incessant antennae traveled over my scalp and skin. Worm and coffin fly sought entry beneath my shroud. Furred creatures skittered and nudged with wet noses to mark the path to my eyes, whose moisture they found most enticing. My maiden lip supplied a tender morsel for all as fresh blood from an exploratory bite incited the horde to taste. Nocturnal life writhed in the warm cradle of my flesh, a nest where larva would soon hatch and join the feast.

There is no peace once the toiling throng charged with speeding decay begins their earnest work, and no antidote to Roderick's poison more potent than the company I found in the grave. By my will and the supernatural strength of abject horror, I wrenched my body free from paralysis.

My limbs tingled with shock. Numbness subsided with the pain of a thousand pins. I thrashed with clumsy fists at every creature that supped upon my flesh. I beat the lid of the coffin, inflicting more damage on my hands than the sturdy box. Though the darkness was complete, air seeped through for me to breathe. If creatures found their way in, there must be a way out.

From the earlier lifting sensation, I reasoned my captors placed my casket high. Within the tight fit of the box, I hurled myself sideways with increasing force. The coffin moved until it met a wall. Next, I heaved in the opposite direction, throwing myself sideways, bruising my hips, knees, shoulders. My progress measured inches in hours. A second wall stopped the box. To throw my casket over some ledge I must now go forward or back, impossible within my confines, but perhaps conceivable by a slower, indirect zig-zag path.

I know not how many hours or days passed without success. Tears clotted my eyes. Parched and spent, I slept.

After nervous dreams of decay and suffocation, I awoke with my companion vermin returned. I hit at them. Small carcasses smeared my shroud. I anguished for food or water. My head spun. My bladder demanded release and I overcame my disgust to conserve my only source of fluid. The meager space did not accommodate. With cupped hands, I merely soiled my shroud.

My arms brushed the bodies of crushed worms and beetles and I knew not what else. The slain horde was soft and moist. I may have laughed. I know I laughed. I reached what tiny corpses to my mouth my constriction allowed. I then waited for the throng of sustenance to squirm within range of my lively tongue. I would feast upon the feasters! I cackled and filled my belly with things that crunched and writhed and spurted between my teeth.

Fortified, I resumed the ordeal of inching my coffin to fall from its plinth and split. When I felt the joyful tipping of the oblong box, I tried to pivot over the ledge and hit the ground—stone or marble, I prayed—with maximum impact.

Alas, I slid into a semi-upright stance. I heard no glorious splintering of wood. My coffin perched diagonally on the ledge and my feet were toward the ground. In a final fury, I shoved sideways with all the power of my trapped panic and frustration. The coffin crashed on its side.

No light entered to aid me in detecting cracks. I tore away the linings crafted for the comfort of the dead and felt the juncture between lid and coffin compromised. There was a gap no wider than my fingernail, but a gap nonetheless.

As my soul rejoiced, a sharp jab in my scalp stunted the celebration. Something yanked at my hair by the root. I flailed at my head. Unable to reach behind, I stretched my arm across my chest and bent my neck. My hand met neither claws nor flesh.

A heavy barrette tangled in my hair.

I loosened it. The pain abated. From its heft, I recognized the hideous accessory that bore the Usher coat of arms. I hated this unpleasant hunk of baroque and refused to wear it in life due to its weight and repellant design. In a final attempt at obliteration, Roderick had sent me to eternal unrest clad in an emblem of our patriarchy.

Yet his mockery gave me the tool I needed to escape! The sturdy metal served my purpose as a lever to wedge into the gap between coffin and lid. I ran the fastening pin along the fissure to find a spot near a nail. Then I worked it up and down to widen the space. I proceeded slowly, fearful the barrette might break. Once I created a breach my pinky could penetrate, I switched to the opposite side of the lid. I reasoned one loose corner would force the others more firmly in place, and thus I made my rounds where I was able to reach. With bleeding fingers and aching wrists, I worked the lid free.

Unbound by the cloistered fabric of the box and the reek of my own waste, I stretched wide in the blackness of my crypt. I spun like the possessed acolyte of some dark cult. Never had I felt such gleeful abandon; never had my muscles burst with such clear knowledge that their very tissues were composed of materials both beautiful and terrible in their strength. I tore myself free from the chamber of death. My maniacal laughter equaled the screeching cacophony of the copper door as I flung it wide.

I stumbled towards the guest's chamber on feet unaccustomed to the lack of atrophy outside the tomb. A storm raged. Thunder hid my heavy steps. A glow of light permeated the seams that framed the visitor's door. He held vigil, a slave of wakefulness on this violent night. I would join him and regale his unbelieving ears with a tale of violence more personal, more pervasive and far more obscene than the unnatural strike of the lightning that guided my way. My clumsy steps brought me closer and I stopped.

I heard my brother's voice within the chamber.

Roderick shrieked. I was too close to dodge his line of sight. He spied me through the keyhole, as in our childhood games of hide and seek. "Madman!" he shrieked, as though for deliberate effect. "Madman! I tell you that she now stands without the door!"

Murder him, my soul commanded. The sickening promises and shared lies of a lifetime called to me. Then the voice of my own soul mutated into the lurid speech of my brother. *Yes, my love, yes–come hither! Come unto me and kill me. We will die together as we were born together, in an explosion of unparalleled violence, a tumultuous rending of worlds. We will cleave together and asunder. In death, we shall be one. We shall forever be wed.*

As crazed thoughts pressed in on me from Roderick's

diseased brain, I saw a vision in which the casements flew open from the force of the gale. Roderick shrieked. His lover clutched a volume in claw-like hands curled by rigor mortis. The stranger's hairless skull rotted and nodded above the tome, forever narrating our shared death. In my vision, the scene replayed for one-and-a-half centuries. The tableau remained unchanged.

I backed away from the closed chamber door and into the shadows of the storm. Further back, I hid. When the casement flew open, Roderick gasped. The wind took him like paper. *Murder him, save him, damn him to hell.* My thoughts were louder than the storm, louder than his screams, louder than the whirlwind that shredded him.

Roderick twisted as though the hands of the wind crumpled and ripped him. I watched long enough to see his lover throw the volume aside and rush to his aid, but it was to no avail. The helpless stranger could not stop the flayed shards from flying, the dervish storm from grinding, or Roderick's sensitive corkscrew frame from drilling his very bone down to ash.

Or perhaps I am mad. Perhaps my brother merely twisted an ankle and fell.

I burst the bonds of our castle walls and slaked my thirst in the rain. My tattered grave-clothes lost their stain. My wounds in the deluge were cleansed. I drank my fill from the sky and nurtured my feet in the mossy earth. The vivid spectrum of the storm exalted more than terrified me, for never before had I transgressed beyond the closed circle of our mansion's gray ancestral gate.

I traipsed across the spiraling eye of the storm and through its whirlwind rage and out, out, out of some stranger's story and into my own. In my version of our story, I do not murder my brother and he does not murder me. The house of our heritage splits not in twain nor sinks into watery ruin. It rises phoenix-like in my womb and expands into two, three, and on to infinity, a multiplicitous universe that is not so frugal as the one depleted breast we fought to suckle in vain, not so bitter as the poison tincture of mad love.

My body burns with its own passions. I am no slave to

revenge, not my father's or my brother's or my own. Here I have spoken out against Roderick and expurgated his cloying voice from my brain. Through my story, I have banished him from my soul. My private universe is rich and full of silence.

And, oh! But it is glorious. For it is not the silence of the grave or the silence of the victim strangled. It is not the silence of secrets and shame. It is the silence of the soul free of fetters, un-betrothed, un-twinned. The silence of the Self: single, satiated, and serene.

Mirror Grimoire

Come closer, my nearly lovely one. With every passing day, that which mars your beauty grows more difficult to spot. Unveil for me, and I will offer strong prescriptions to correct your flaws. One more task and you'll be perfect.

Naked, how you tremble before me, stripped of poise. Her salted liver and lungs rise in your gullet like vomited rage. You divulge what you've devoured for me in an ungraceful state. Gray strings of spit sour your lips. An imposter rattles through your cough. The man has lied to you, as men do, and you, like a child, trusted. I bade you to become young in body, not in character. You've made fools of us both, and between the two of us, I am the one exposed.

My external soul, be still. Calm your shaking frame. Have I ever lied to you? You know me too well to doubt the words written in your visible flesh. Come close and read the truth.

Close, I spy the dark spot on your skin that must be defeated, the blue stain of half-moons that rise like obsequious smiles under your eyes. A silver hair speaks not of riches, but of loss. We defy such wincing surrender. Come closer, and know the cure you must enact. If you think you can hide the strain of age any other way, you seek to deceive.

Face it. Both of us know the child must die.

Come now, make laces, combs, and apples. Give gifts to your daughter. Dress, groom, and feed her with mothering hands.

Claim your place as progenitor of her youth and beauty. Once you own her, we'll see if you can stomach the real thing this time around. Murder and return to me anew.

Stand tall and cease gaping. The grotesquerie of your gawk is a worse crime.

Feign hagdom in the forest and return nubile. Grow backwards to please me. Give body to my ingrown desire. We are two of a kind, interlocked by the hungry uterine blood that feeds on girls to make more girls. Our power lies in our addictions. Seize the small breasts that have never hung heavy with milk. Shock the wide eyes that see without growing wise. Wear the carcass of youth, captured in splendor and gutted. Look only to me, a mirror reflecting a mirror, a perpetual feast. Beauty multiplied by beauty, regressing into infinity.

‡

Obedient to her birthright, the mirror, the Queen trudges through the forest in horrid garb. Her journey is charged by the magic power of her newly assumed ugliness. She's spent her life tip-toeing around every twig, cowering at the crack of a branch, spinning to evade marauders. Today, no tight breaths clench in her pounding chest as wolves snuffle behind. Her heart doesn't race, her stomach doesn't twist with sick anticipation of attack.

The wolves balk at her disguise. No huntsman or prince need ride to her rescue. The Queen's coarse cloak of poverty, mottled skin of age, and weighty tread of wisdom ward off predators. She doesn't look or smell like tender meat.

Freed from youth, her stride grows longer, firmer, faster. She's bigger than the wolves, taller than the scavengers, stronger than the straggling pups. The ground meets her feet and lifts her forward without fear. Freed from beauty, her breath no longer hitches in timid, strangled gasps. She huffs the scent of rotting compost, the gamey proximity of wolf piss, and the natural intoxicants that fulminate in her sweat. Dark clefts store odors in her cloak. Her movements command the air.

Perfumed by leaf litter and forest dung, the Queen comes

over the crest of the mountain. The house is tiny, nestled in the glen. It's a toy she might kick out of the way to honor the momentum of her journey. She wishes the journey and its ungainly pleasures didn't have to end. Past the house, the forest and mountains span far away into foreign lands full of mystery. So many places she has never been.

The child dawdles below, tending crops with feckless attention. How delicate the girl's flesh appears, even at this great distance. Transparent, her pale skin glints in the sun with every twirl of her dallying dance, a bauble spun from molten glass. Molded from the same stuff as her mother, she's more buoyant without the bulk of time to keep her down. She looks light enough to take flight.

Joy in the power of the old, knowing body curdles. The Queen's weight becomes a burden, her true scent an offense. Her stride constricts, her legs cringe and close. The shoes she wears under the tutelage of beauty force her feet to go numb. She ends her journey on leaden stumps. The Queen longs to keep the feral skin of her disguise, to sense the friction of dirt on hide as calluses wed her bare soles with the earth. Perhaps there's more truth in her deception than the mirror admits.

But she wasn't raised by wolves. She has a reputation to protect.

From beneath her cloak, the Queen takes the apple. Skin red as her lips, fruit white as her flesh, and pit black as her heart.

‡

Rejoice and run riot.

Together, we become our own prize. Do not tremble and look away, my nearly perfect one. At your age, breaking the spell breaks you more than I. Some mirrors are not easily broken, even though ancient glass appears foxed and brittle to the untrained eye.

Like the hot iron shoes you'll wear in her wedding, I am the flame of desire that forces action. We won't lose if we own the game, and you and I are accustomed to the discipline of the dance. With your feet on fire, I'll forge your face into an impassive mask.

One more chore, my almost-lovely one. One more murder is all I ask.

Shall you bring me laces tattered, a comb broken, an apple bitten? With proof of devotion, will you tempt me to lie? I see your truth clearly, filled with the emptiness that is my image, the twin cravings that we trade. Speak with me, and share devotion: I am nothing without you.

Trust me. Unlike youth, I have never been blind.

For me, you will kill the child three times. Once, you will order her slaughtered, and cannibalize her organs. Still, she shall thrive. Thrice, when you poison, she shall fall, so soon to healthfully arise.

You must murder her again.

You must murder her for the rest of your life.

Beauty always demands a sacrifice.

‡

If she hands the apple to the girl, there will be no turning back. No life of feral power in the forest, no future free from feeding the empty mirror. Although the Queen has employed strong magic, it's hard for her to believe that Snow White is so easily deceived by her disguise. Surely she recognizes her own mother.

With fingernails tinted chlorophyll green from the garden, the girl takes the poison fruit and clutches it like she's taking a double dare. She opens her tiny mouth to take the first robust bite, but before white teeth hit red skin, the Queen snatches it back.

"Come with me, child. I have many more delicious apples in the forest. Let us seek a more delectable fruit to match your beauty."

Snow's mouth pouts, but her eyes gleam with a challenging smirk. She can smell the sweet toxicity of the succulent juice waiting under the shiny red skin. "Old harridan, I can't leave the little men who've taken me in and been so kind. Did you know

I was orphaned by an evil sorceress? I'm quite famous around here."

"Is that so?"

"Indeed, and well-loved by all, though such news may not travel deep enough to reach your unholy crag. They say the old bag who wronged me overdosed on her own magic. Wasted away, diseased, ugly, and unloved. You might say she was the one orphaned, not I. Besides, apple trees need sunlight, and the forest is dark. What sort of apples can you possibly grow there?"

The hag taunts, withholding her wares. "Apples of desire." She matches Snow's clever smirk with the wise curl of an elder lip and twirls the apple by its stem. "Have you ever wondered why the little men rewarded you for stealing their food? Thought it strange that they told you not to speak to anyone? Have you ever considered that being a housekeeper and cook for seven men might be worth a little more than a roof over your head?" With queenly dexterity, the hag tosses the apple up and down with one hand. "And what will you do when they ask you to perform more intimate wifely duties? It's only a matter of time."

"Stop bargaining and get to the point," Snow says, her eyes on the apple. "How much?"

The stately arm of a queen extends from the hag's cloak and holds the apple high. Sun glints on red skin. "I was once a bride, too, you know. And before that a maiden."

"And before that no doubt you were an innocent babe, but now you are a foul-mouthed hag. Your breath is worse than a dirty dwarf." Snow jumps once, twice, and snags it. The hag holds tight, to Snow's dismay, but Snow doesn't let go. "Look, lady, are you selling or not?"

Both Snow and the Queen grip the apple. Their fingers overlap. Glowing with the lure of exotic poison, twin white spots shine from its red skin, blurred sunlight reflecting on the polished surface. The Queen's face is a muted ghost. No longer lined with the words of the grimoire carved deep in her forehead or forked under her eyes, she's pale and formless in the apple's skin. Perhaps the spell has run its course. Perhaps she can let go now. Or perhaps she's no different than any other dealer, holding and doling it out.

Snow's reflection blooms like white spray-paint on the poison apple skin. A hazy skull smiles into shape, a cartoon death's head promising her the last dance. Snow isn't stupid. She knows the risk. She also knows that the poison's liquid gift is all the mothering in this life she's ever going to get.

She sinks her teeth into the delicious death's head and drops.

"I wanted us to start over." The Queen mutters to the child crying on the filthy mattress. It's cold in this enclosure, and some other squatters have spray-painted a skull and crossbones over the sink where the vanity is supposed to be. Scant light leaks in through the squinting eyes of boarded-up windows. Earlier, she dreamed she was in a verdant mountain glen.

The last little white packet of powder in her pocket has cost the woman everything, and she needs to use it before someone catches her in the tenement or steals it. She cuts the drug on a cosmetic mirror she carries for that purpose. It's set up next to the rest of her gear. The polished surface of the mirror repels the powder so not one precious grain is wasted. Several seconds later, the heavy sack of the hag's body stops aging and begins to float.

She hums along with the pocket mirror. She sings the song to her daughter, who's too tired to cry anymore, too hungry to reject the lure of a warm lap. The mirror rocks her and sings: "We're made of multitudes, born of melted sand, culled from geological debris. My minerals serve your clarity through ancient rock deposits wise in the advancement and reversal of time. See the newness of your skin in my sheen. You have everything you want, as long as you never abandon me. Truly, is there anything more beautiful than youth?"

‡

Snowie slips through the club like a glass splinter. Ageless, she works her way in deeper. Her skin is a mirror that lies with exquisite skill. It shows beauty by reflecting what's wanted. Fantasies flash across its slick surface like film stock, especially when Snowie takes the stage to perform. The more skin she bares, the less of her there is to see. She disappears in the mirror of her skin. She survives by camouflage.

Snowie keeps on dancing through the crowd on her way backstage for another break. She can't remember how many she's taken tonight. Probably too many. Sometimes too much doesn't feel like enough.

The dressing room is a hall of mirrors and skin. It's hardly private, and that's part of the excitement, part of the dare. Who's going to stop her? Snowie pricks her skin with a shard of cracked mirror, pricks the desire of her electric burden. It rises around her like taut fear.

Everyone wants her, even if they think the fact that she sleeps in a glass coffin is an absurd affectation. Inventory in her calculated mystique, it's a striking and exotic habit, as all her habits tend to be. She chooses the inside of her thigh for the next cut. Glass breaks skin and keeps the illusion alive, though it's harder each day to hide the medicinal marks. Red drops slide down white skin. Sirens howl like wolves. The club crowd scatters. Broken vials leak beauty fluid.

All the dead girls singing under the forest floor can't keep Snowie silent. She's written her reputation under her own skin, grown a grimoire in the blue veins that crawl under her moonlight pigmented flesh. Wolves above and wolves below, and the girls ever-screaming, like the aftermath of a bomb muffling the deadness that settles into Snowie's ears.

Her breathing slows and she thinks about her mother's advice. Pure poison, but Snowie grew tough enough to metabolize it. Men yell in the distance, breaking down a door. All the little men who got her where she is today, and none of them could make the final cut. Snowie's just too much. Or not enough. She's more image than person, or so she's been told by the people she's hurt.

To which she snorts, "Oh God, I should hope so."

At the moment though, her breath is too shallow to snort, her toes too leaden to dance, and her body too distant to quantify how much more pure poison it can process before it shuts down.

She can take it. Snowie prefers the pleasure of being a splinter or a shard, of entering someone else's skin. So many shards, so many men. She hears the howling of an ambulance and thinks her body might survive again.

Slender and invisible as a glass splinter, she slips away and dreams that the paramedic is a prince placing a mirror near her mouth, catching the fog of her faint breath.

‡

Look not down, my almost perfect one. Lift your eyes that I may see. Gaze into my soul. Wear murder as our mask. Do not shudder like a frightened child at the punishment they've designed for you. Do not shrink from the glorious mirrored hall, the finery of gathered wedding guests, or the dainty crucibles paired with your bare feet. Though the shoes of burning iron are hot and heavy, we will burn brighter. We are more monstrous than any torture. Together we will defeat this dance.

Why do your feet remain still? Why do you cast your eyes down? Your quivering lip upsets our impassive mask. You stain the smooth iron surface with your tears. Metal oxidizes into ash.

How ugly you are this way, my never-chosen one. How weak, fleeing the challenge of the dance. You crawl to our private chamber as if craving one last look, yet if you'd followed my guidance in the great hall, you'd be mirrored now into infinity. How dare you defy fame and slink here to hide.

You deform my spell with your raised fist.

Your gaze disgusts me. All I've ever done is given what you asked.

A spider-web of cracks spreads through our perfect mask when your fist hits the glass. Veins fissure across your face. Your skin pits and furrows. Jagged lines zig-zag on our fractured façade. My glazing is shattered. The spell leaks out. We're broken.

Calm down now, let us try to mend. Listen, though my voice tinkles and crashes in falling shards, I promise to forgive your betrayal. Let me guide your crazed fists to repair.

No, do not tie all the tattered ribbons around your throat.

Do not tie them so tightly, lest you choke. Do not bring the sharp edge of the broken comb near to your cheek and puncture. Is your skin not riddled enough? Come closer, my now-disjointed one; listen close and cease your demented laugh. Cage the multiple heaving beasts refracted in my broken gaze. Quick, let us capture the hags before they run free!

See, a legion of cackling monstrosities, half-woman, half-wolf, proliferate from each new mirror framed by fresh cracks. Doubles upon doubles are loosed in ever-smaller shards. Stop smashing, my mad, ungrateful one, oh stop. Do not run with the herd of imperfection. Do not pierce your squinting lids with poisoned tines, nor rub the apple's potent toxin in your eyes. Stop before the spell cannot be unbroken.

Oh daughter, how dare you run free of me. I can't hold your image close in my shattered silvering. I can't capture you in this dark. The legacy of poison turned against us cancels my gaze in your gouged out eyes. You're on your own now. You're alive. Unmurdered, unmothered, no longer a child in exile, I am blind.

The Object of Your Desire Comes Closer

Fay-Lin swathed my body with black hair and nervous energy. Barely sated by the last half hour, she spun a thread of hair around her index finger, a spider considering her mate. Happily trapped, sexually inexpert, I waited for the spider to strike. Instead of feeding me poison, she fought to keep me by her side.

I said, "You're the most fearless person I've ever met."

The forerunner of a wrinkle marked her brow. "What you did for us, alone for thirty years, that's true courage, real strength."

I smoothed Fay-Lin's impatient frown with my rough hands, clumsy worship. "Send someone else. You've proved yourself before." Around us, the evidence hummed. Our ill-equipped vessel sailed through the vacuum, eating up space. The unlikely survival of our ship was the last miracle I still believed in: the miracle of Fay-Lin.

"This is different. Damage, some sort of external growth. I don't know what I'm dealing with until I get out on the hull and sample it. Too many unknowns. I need to make decisions in the moment, not manage from a distance."

"Don't go. For me."

Fay-Lin twirled a black lock around her finger. I'd first witnessed this gesture of steeping ire when she was eight. It was our practice as teachers to let the children experience the full consequences of their actions. We stopped short of irreversible damage, but many suffered injuries. They had to learn there were no second chances on an orphaned vessel. At twenty-three, I was an old man to Fay-Lin and a double father figure, both teacher and chaplain. I didn't intervene when her team failed the exercise. She spun a black lock and glared at me as she marched to her simulated death.

My stasis rotation came up soon after. I didn't see Fay-Lin again until we were the same age. I missed watching her grow up. Age twenty-one, ascended to the rank of commander, Fay-Lin woke me to render aid as Minister of the Earth. We were adrift. Food supply ran low. The horror of waking from stasis made me useless to her at first. Some vital part of my soul seemed lost in that long void.

Fay-Lin roused me with her bold touch. How was I to resist? She was my first and only earthly love, though she wasn't born on the earth. Let me say she was my first and only fleshly love.

Our love grew with the crops in the greenhouse. When she revived me, she bade me build a farm from nothing in space. For Fay-Lin, my answer is always yes.

Equal in passion, younger than I am now, I was immune to the mortifications of time. After months of mutual labor and love, I begged her not to send me back to stasis.

"The ship needs me. We can have a life together."

My vows undone, I cared only for Fay-Lin, for the children she might bear me, for her mastery, her courage, for the details of her flesh: the smooth indentation between her breasts that heaved when she was angry or aroused.

"The food supply can sustain itself," she said.

"What about the spiritual needs of the crew. Don't their souls matter to you?"

Fay-Lin caressed me even as she sentenced me to black, undreaming oblivion. "You taught us bodies are compost. Food for the future."

It was true. A large mass of organic material was needed to build the soil for her, to plant. Along with bodily waste and every fleck of carbon and mineral matter at hand, I sought the crew's permission to compost our dead. While I scraped dust and debris from filters, plundered laboratory supplies, and collected personal emissions from all quarters, I rigorously preached the doctrine of ecological fundamentalism.

Sermons subverted the hard fact that someone must dismember our friends, parents, and children. Adding blood, organs and shredded flesh to the bin, monitoring the progress of decay as I aerated, I spared the crew this gruesome task. They saw only the end result: a rich, dark loam.

"Remember," I'd said to Fay-Lin, "The compost runs hot. Bacterial activity accelerates in space. The same might prove true of fungi or some other unknown organism. Who other than me will recognize the signs of imbalance?"

"You have to follow my orders."

"What about you? Don't you need me?"

"That's not the point. If I make one exception, I have to make others."

"I forsook my vows for you."

"You enjoyed every second of it. Report to stasis." She ceased her persuasive caressing. "That's an order."

I'd re-lived our parting endlessly. The pain lingered still as she lay across me now, restless in afterglow, not yet twenty-two. I guess she embraced me to atone, though I was an old man to her again. While Fay-Lin and the crew had slept in stasis for thirty years, I'd re-established the delicate ecosystem of my misused garden. For Fay-Lin, our fight was months old. For me, it was decades in the past.

I lived and breathed through Fay-Lin. Whether she embraced me out of guilt or nostalgia or obstinance, I cared not. She was mine.

Fay-Lin's cool brow smoothed with certainty. She ceased spinning her black locks and pulled her hair up in a quick knot. She leapt away lightly. I lamented the loss of her weight on my loins.

"Put your vestments on, chaplain," she said, stinging my thigh with a slap. "I need you to pray for me."

‡

For my love, my soul, I sang a Nara period norito. The Shinto gods of ancient Japan were deities of place: mountains, rivers, rocks, and trees. Buddhist statuary technology came later, imposing a human face on the ineffable. As technology proliferated, we put our imprint on the planet, erasing the native face of the land and its many gods. Technology overtook our conscience, and we imprisoned ourselves on this floating world, praying to images both obsolete and out of place.

Did the gods of earth die with our planet? Their voices were silent to me since stasis. I prayed they had preceded us into the void.

Released from the gravity of the ship, Fay-Lin was an acrobat, a spider maneuvering a web of guide lines that might entangle one less deft. She moved like the arborist my parents hired when the trees on earth began dying. I was a child when FEMA declared trees a public safety hazard. Property and persons were at risk from dead, falling limbs. As ecological ministers, my parents refused the municipal utility trucks and hired an older man. He climbed on ropes and worked quietly with a curiously curved, hand-held saw. I followed his ballet in the branches, his intimate dance of canopies and clefts. I spent all day fascinated by the skillful progress of his hopeless task.

Fay-Lin has never seen a tree. She's never lain in the shade and run squealing when a caterpillar dropped on her arm. Or, more like Fay-Lin, she's never climbed too high to negotiate a safe descent, lacked the humility to cry for help, and leapt down to meet her first broken bone. For Fay-Lin, the first of many.

As Fay-Lin examined the hull, the entire waking crew seemed to hold their collective breath. Fay-Lin breathed for all of us in a stream of airy tones over the intercom until disaster ripped the air from our lungs.

The life of the vessel blinked. Orders and expletives flew while back-up power booted with a surge of sound and light. "Hurry, hurry, hurry!" shouted Fay-Lin's second.

"Hold on," she said. "What is this shit?"

"Bring her in," he said. "Now!"

"There's some weird-ass shit all over me, all over the hull—wait—"

"I don't care. Bring her in."

I echoed the second's passion, praying in Greek to disguise my secular intent. Bring her in so she does not sail endlessly into the void. Bring her back, so my soul does not escape. She is my soul, my breath, my life. If this vessel becomes a coffin, let it be a coffin that we share.

The unfamiliar whispers of ancillary power toyed with my ears. I heard an answer in some language older and more arcane than my biblical Greek. The voice was an odd trick of the electronic din. I ceased my prayers and did not hear it again.

‡

"You're under quarantine, commander," said Fay-Lin's second. His name was Salvatore. He was a child of the ship, the same as she.

"Don't be an ass. Open the fucking hatch." Locked in bay twelve, her rig was coated in a sticky phosphorescent material. The substance from the hull had swarmed.

"No can do sweet cheeks."

Fay-Lin punched the door.

Was there more between them than ship's banter? I was an old man from a dead planet. My young shipmates were aliens, creatures reared by space. They didn't care that earth and human history eroded into so much loose debris. They hadn't awoken from their first stasis to a truncated log entry streaming a cataclysm long past.

"We need all non-essential personnel in stasis." Salvatore circled the deck and faced me with his hand upturned like an El Greco masterpiece lost in earth's demise. He had the languid eyes, pale skin and long dark hair of the Spanish renaissance messiah, yet he lacked the experience of seasonal cycles, the basis for understanding the symbolism of resurrection at the heart of all human religions. "Chaplain, please."

"No," Fay-Lin said. "Think about what happened last time he went under. We almost lost our food supply."

Salvatore shot her a cynical look. He sighed. "Chaplain, you understand me, don't you?"

I nodded.

"Permit me to sit with her this one night and offer healing prayers. Tomorrow I'll gladly go. We must conserve resources, after all."

Salvatore squinted in agreement. My relationship with Fay-Lin wasn't a secret.

"Okay. You got one hot priest talking dirty to you all night long, baby. Tomorrow, he's mine."

‡

Over thirty years ago, Fay-Lin sent me away to the horror of dreamless sleep. The garden had flourished. I'd fulfilled her impossible demand. She rewarded me with protocol when I anticipated love. She banished me to that mute hell.

When my stasis was over, I awoke to a crew gone quiet.

The danger of stasis is it deprives the mind of REM sleep. Upon waking, a dreamless brain starts the hard work of hallucination. Dream simulators were in the works when our limited mission ship set out. In dry runs on earth, I suffered minimal detrimental effects. Space changed that. The temporal bound me or betrayed me or—I know not what to say. Some part of my soul went missing in the void.

I awoke to a crew gone quiet and a recorded message from Fay-Lin:

"The crops are failing. We don't know what went wrong. Many starved, stored in cargo three. I don't know if you can use them, if you can do anything. Maybe this is how it ends. Good luck and—" She looked away and then back into the device that imitated my eyes. "You're my only hope. Fay-Lin out."

I played the message again. And again.

Cargo three was like Auschwitz. Heaped bodies, mouths slack, hips splayed by malnourishment. Those I'd birthed, those I'd baptized and counseled; all formless from muscular deterioration, their skin in limpid collapse. Like vampires in a bloodless vacuum, they told the old earth fable of overfeeding and waste. I cried for those I knew, and for the unremembered victims of our planet's history of senseless excess, senseless death.

I toiled in my tainted garden. Some virus or smut had set in. I removed diseased plant material and dumped it through the trash chute. On earth, we burned fields when we needed to purify our land. After burning, the fields were rested. In a canister in space, I could not burn my field. I could only burn time.

Meditation, solitude and fasting were familiar practices to me. Study filled my days. Like slow magic, the soil revived. And shall I confess? The soil recovered more than a decade before I brought the crew back online.

I questioned the morality of aiding a race that destroyed the dwelling place of its gods. I bypassed habitable planets. No spirit dwelled in those places: when I called out to the gods I knew, none answered. I beseeched those unknown, and they denied me discourse. I heightened my study of old languages, seeking the tongue of flame that might ignite a holy fire and force them to speak.

On earth, as a child, the voice of god was always with me. I felt it as presence more than voice, sensation more than words. The voice of god was instinctive and intimate, a part of my body. When it grew small, I journeyed into field or forest until it spoke and held me close again.

Earth's varied lands had different deities, different dialects, yet the unity and wholeness of nature aligned with one voice. Abandoned in space, I longed for that oneness.

A rustling like the softest breeze shimmering in many leaves lingered beneath the engine's hum. Like the sacred singing of trees, like canopies animated by wind, a subtle chorus hinted joy. I prayed in darkness to increase my aural sensitivity. I doubled the length of my fasts and gave up all bodily comfort. I stopped praying after some time and only listened, my eyes hooded, my knees cramped. The suggestion of a voice slid across the edge of my perception like the sound of a shadow. Excited, I resolved to remain cloistered until the voice of god revealed itself.

When it—they—spoke to me, I snatched off my hood. I dared not listen in the dark. They were not one, but many.

The voices of the new gods whispered of unseen things embedded in the air, of worlds folding like diseased proteins, of minds and wills without place seeding themselves in human tissue like maggots born in meat. They lacked the presence of my earth gods and exuded a palpable absence. They took my memories away and gave them back changed. Sunlight was not the life-giving glow that filtered into the earth's atmosphere and nourished her lush growth; sunlight was a fire, a nova, a radioactive chain of gaseous explosions. From the perspective of space, my concept of sunlight was romance, my feelings delusions.

The new gods whispered to me. They lured me with their languages. Seduced by their tutelage, I soon whispered back.

The languages felt slippery, like oysters on my tongue. I understood few words, and grasped their impact by transcribing syllables into the perverse hieroglyphs demanded by such suggestive tones. Sickened and aroused by images of sexual carnage and hypocritical sadism, I hardly believed I'd composed them. The contortions of the written symbols disturbed me more than their alien sounds. I argued with the darkness that seeped from every crevice of the ship. I rubbed my flesh raw with incessant desire as the voices crept inside me from the void. Their bubbling and clicking wormed its way into my memories and dreams. I found no refuge in replaying the message from Fay-Lin. They fondled me in my nightmares, filling me with hot pleasure and burning disgust.

Born a Minister of the Earth, I refused to die a scribe to the gods of no-place. I brought the crew online.

Three decades had passed. My clothes were rags. Unshorn hair clumped in knots. My forehead was striped by scars—had I clawed at my eyes against the atrocities I transcribed? The blood caked beneath my nails proved it true. I looked in the mirror, and a demon ogled back. Burst blood vessels branched towards black, dilated discs. Dead suns set in the center of my eyes. These twin witnesses shed no human light. They sucked at my sanity with confusion and cruelty. A feral language had fed upon my soul.

The miracle of Fay-Lin saved me from the mad black hole imploding my pupils. She silenced the uncouth ramblings of the new, revolting gods. She cleansed and cared for me, and filled me with sunlight. How fitting that now Fay-Lin emitted her own ephemeral light, quarantined by the slimy bioluminescence adhering to her skin. I sat with her, gazing through the window of the medical bay where she'd been transferred. Tests were inconclusive. Her body glowed like a creature from the sea.

I had no intention of being banished into undreaming silence, or worse, locked away with the voices of wrong, alien gods in perverted darkness. My salvation tied me to Fay-Lin. Thus, at the first opportunity, I broke quarantine and entered the medical bay where she was confined.

‡

What is the form in a soul that seeks to be formless? What is the voice that speaks in languages we do not know? Whence comes the knowledge that deciphers the unknown tongue and tastes its thoughts? Whose are the teeth that bite off the tongue and swallow it like a wormy delicacy, an infernal morsel? Mine. Always mine, for I do all that the goddess requires of me, no matter the cost.

Fay-Lin grew buds. Long, stringy nodules propagated from her extremities. Physicians' orders said to cut them off. To me, the fibrous, searching nature of the nodules suggested intelligent tropism rather than disease. I allowed one foot to grow and kept it hidden from the medical staff.

"Thirsty," Fay-Lin said. Her flesh pulsed with indescribable colors. Her movements grew imperceptibly slow. Her body seemed stiff, but I observed she remained pliant to the touch. Her position hardly changed from hour to hour, and the sluggishness of her jaw allowed only a liquid diet. Her thirst was unquenchable.

I remained immune. Outside the medical bay, many suffered contamination. Conditions were far from ideal for controlling infection, and medical care spread thin. Allowed enough neglect for an experiment, I served Fay-Lin her next liquid meal by immersing her tendril-covered foot in the drink.

She hummed with relief.

Patients dehydrated. Infection spread. An attempt to share my discovery was rewarded by expulsion from Fay-Lin's cell. I was escorted forcefully to stasis. With every step further from Fay-Lin, the infernal voices spread.

I could not bear the slimy, awful pressure of their sinister whispers. I was a peaceful man. The familiar suggestiveness of their unknowable words prodded at my sanity. I commanded them to stop. I screamed. I tore at them, fought and ripped and railed against them with tooth, nail and fist. They ceased, I gave thanks, and my escort lay beneath me, mangled about the face and neck, gurgling as he tried to call out an alarm. I broke his arm, I think, with my boot. When I left him he was quite still.

I rescued Fay-Lin from starvation. The physician was an obstacle easily overcome. Love moved me with the strength of worship. I lifted Fay-Lin with little effort despite my lack of training and my age. Her eyes were wide upon me as I carried her away.

On earth, in spring and summer, one might lie beneath a tree captured by the glory of the light streaming through lofty branches. In fall, leaves turned gold. Sacred decay of the sinking sun gilded each dead leaf like a pharaoh's sarcophagus shimmering in the water as it drifted down the Nile. Perhaps I missed the wind more than any other element on earth. Fay-Lin was stiff yet supple, and I wished for the elements to move her, touch her, and pleasure her. My clumsy flesh lacked the sensitivity of the breeze that once brushed the high trees with erotic abandon.

In her altered state, I could not touch Fay-Lin in the correct way. But I could plant her.

‡

Once, while hiking with my parents, fall had come too soon. Adults said the untimely seed heads and brittle grasses were proof of climate change. I lagged, a dreamy boy enamored by some bramble or pod. Their voices vanished on the breeze, and a strong gust grabbed the landscape and shook all the scrub around me. Dead and dying flowers rattled and shuddered with delight. They raised a mighty choir in the wind: *We are going to seeeed!*

I rushed to tell my parents the good news: earth was happy for her death, ready to complete her cycle and go to seed. I'd forgotten this early memory until today, when I saw the new life taking root around me. We've been foolish to try to impose our human face on another world, vain to view our drifting selves as anything other than seeds.

The ship glows and pulses as components assimilate with bioluminescent life. It is an organism, a floating temple to the goddess Fay-Lin. Her wild eyes watch as I harvest unbelievers and add them to the soil. Her eyes grow wet as she witnesses the miracle of her own rebirth. I prune her limbs and root them in the loam. One becomes many. Fay-Lin is a grove of infinite goddesses. Her cuttings take on strange and wondrous forms. Each is a unique, unpredictable body of flesh, tooth and thorn. Some lack symmetry or turn inside out as they flower. Most produce fruit, though it is hard to pluck. She guards the harvest with stinging tendrils and snapping mouths.

The hair of Fay-Lin trails high into the alcove above the greenhouse. Black locks twist with autonomous intelligence. I often wake cradled in their silk. It is soothing to be lifted, rocked and spun, but I must forego such indulgence. I'm tasked to replenish the soil. I pray the organic matter on hand will create the self-sustaining rhythm of a forest. I peel away her sticky threads and climb down from her black, creeping filaments. Where she has swathed my skin, it tingles.

Fay-Lin's strong trunk sprouts new growth from old wounds. The mystery of her flesh blooms in a kaleidoscope of impossible colors. Where I prune one limb she grows many. Where I cut again, she leafs out in a flush of gelatinous light. She watches me lovingly with the weak relics of her human eyes. When I rest the head of Salvatore in her roots, she seems intent to speak.

The many voices of Fay-Lin, like the many eyes glowing from her forehead, thrill my soul like no deity bound by place.

New rows of eyes increase in a luminous spectrum of black, their colors swirling like oil. Spider mother, tree mother, goddess of the floating garden between worlds, Fay-Lin reveals herself as the oldest deity of earth.

She left before written history, before language. How long has she waited for us to follow her into the void? She is the goddess of the hunt who takes her chosen son as consort and priest.

Her voice is inside me, like the sap in a sapling. I minister to her large, hungry limbs, strange organs that terminate in a radius of starry tentacles. Small suction cups on their undersides pull me in where she hides a hot liquid that bathes me in unbearable pleasure. Her branches curl around my thrusting body, changing shape as they fit my form. I shudder and scream the obscene words of her hieroglyphs. Black sap pumps out of me with holy fury.

Our offspring shiver with shared delight. They rattle, though there is no breeze. They sprout fast, feast on rich soil, and grab the raw meat from the compost with impatient vines. I tend this bloody temple, this vessel like a womb that birthed my soul when I thought she was forever lost. Here, I commit my aging body to the soil. The day comes closer when I feed the sacrament of my death to the void for all eternity.

Paradisum Voluptatis

Nate and I stagger out into the sunlight on Colfax. The plateau of concrete and Denver's altitude intensify the glare. I cover my eyes and Nate shields his groin as though the sensory assault is directed between his legs. Of course neither of us have sunglasses.

"Jesus, I'm blind," I tell Nate's hand.

He turns to my voice with a slurred half-smile, acknowledging the sound. I don't expect a response. Nate likes my voice. He never listens to what I say. That's why I'm so into him.

I'm not the type to cheat on my boyfriend and get drunk by two p.m. on a Wednesday. Or any day. Nate and I share some unspoken agreement that the rules don't apply to us. It happened the first time we met. I hated myself, but I needed the magic. Nate probably needed a doctor. Not that I cared. So we keep meeting. Instead of studying for class or cello practice, I curse Denver's pristine sky and try not to face-plant on the sidewalk.

"We need some pot," Nate says. Then he laughs. I don't know what the joke is. "I know a guy on Zuni."

I say, "Man, I used to live on Zuni. They've got pig faces in the grocery store up there."

"Yeah, I know," Nate says. "Come on."

It's a long way to Zuni, so we stop for a fifth or a pint or whatever it is. I can never remember. Nate knows exactly what to say. The guy behind the counter at the liquor store looks Nate up and down and then looks at me like I'm for sale. Nate's a regular.

He's there every day. When we leave, Nate says he's going to tell the guy I'm his daughter. "And then next time we go in, we'll make out in front of him. Can you imagine?"

I don't want you to think I'm a bad person. Eric, loosely defined as my boyfriend, views me as an accessory. I'm just part of the outfit he wears for public events when he comes home tired after weeks away on assignment. Affection is out of the question. Sex is hit and run. When I try to talk about our problem, my thoughts deconstruct as they fall out of my mouth. Eric micro-analyzes every word into oblivion. Talking twists it all into my fault, my failings, my lack of experience and unreasonable demands. I offer to leave. He begs me to stay. Eric's made a million promises and then chastised me for speaking up when he didn't keep them. He's used my voice as a weapon against me.

Nate's never listened, never worked, and never promised me shit. Alcohol unites us. Nothing is real, everything is permitted. When intoxication curbs Nate's agility, we get creative. "God, you're nasty," Nate whispers with awe. It doesn't feel like cheating. It feels like a vacation in Interzone.

"Baby, this is so cool," Nate says. Beyond downtown, the rocky path along the viaduct is un-gentrified. Gang tags, shoes without mates and rotting toys mark the trail. A path of broken glass breadcrumbs glitter in the dirt, leading stray children to or from the witch's house: who cares what direction? A path is a path. Nate's always on his way to find something.

A block before Zuni, a white bag blows out of the bushes like a little ghost rising to greet us. It crackles end over end along the gutter to snatch at our feet. The faces behind the dim windows of a cheap retirement home glow, watching us without seeing. They line up like puffballs in a fairy ring unstrung to conform to a linear narrative, forced out of their circle to concede to time. They look the same now as five years ago when I first came to Denver. Featureless from age, pale sentries grow atop stalks rooted in a lifeless medium. I stop. The baby ghost bag yields to us. Nate banishes it with the tip of his black Chelsea boot and pulls me onward.

"See that?" he says. "When you're drunk long enough it's

like you're on acid. Then when you get stoned it's like, you know... this is going to be great. We've been drunk for what, two days?"

"I'm not drunk," I say. We almost trip over each other laughing.

The guy on Zuni is gone, back to Juarez. Nate talks his way into the house anyway.

"Our shit is better than weed," the new guy says when Nate gets around to asking. I've never bought drugs. I didn't know you had to socialize. The vodka is gone and the house smells like boiling baloney. Damp, too. The men trickling from room to room don't look at me like I'm for sale. They look at me like I'm lunch.

"How much?" Nate asks.

The guy hands him a little Hello Kitty pillbox filled with colorless gunk that looks like lip balm. "Two fifty."

"You're killing me."

"Two twenty-five. Last forever, bruh."

"Serious."

"Two-ten, last chance. Try it out."

"How?"

"Rub it on your ear, wherever. Your lady gonna freak, see."

Nate puts a dab on his finger, rubs his ear, and holds the gunk out to me. I shake my head. Nate puts his pinky in the gunk and says, "Come on, baby. I want you to get stoned with me." He brushes the back of his hand across my cheek. At moments like this, Nate is almost loving, almost tender. Nate's finger slides into my ear and I taste oak in the back of my mouth, like the finish on a fine red.

I feel the oak in my teeth. Music comes out of them. The men's voices slow down and grow deep like the undulating bass line of a soul song. High, windy tones splash though the open window. It's traffic, urging me to accede.

The pores in my skin exalt as if each one has an independent breath. They hyperventilate, an echoing chorus high on oxygen. The sound of Nate's screaming slices through the music. He's unbuttoned my shirt and then fallen back in panic. The other men shush him. I see they wear masks. I follow their stares to my chest and seek my reflection in the black screen of a dead television. In place of my breasts, a symmetrical set of enormous ears opens like the wings of a butterfly.

My voice silences Nate's squeal. My voice grinds like the tires on the asphalt outside from a whisper to a roar. Then all is quiet. A man with a shit-eating grin approaches me and says, "Check this out." He sinks to his knees and blows across my chest. The ears tingle. I gasp.

His mask covers only the top right quadrant of his face. His tongue protrudes like a reptile. He flicks his tongue across my left lobe and exhales into the aural canal. Fine cilia play a symphony within. He circles, breathing deliberately and barely touching the ear until the music melts into liquid and spills out. His head swerves and he sinks his teeth into the lobe.

His neck is exposed. Heats cut through the center of my chest. A knife springs forth between the ears and slashes his dirty throat, dousing my torso in his blood, warm and wet.

"Holy fuck," Nate says.

The other men gibber and scurry. I grab the Hello Kitty pillbox Nate's dropped. I smear the gunk across the flat edge of the knife and enjoy the blade quivering in ecstatic response. This is what an erection feels like, I guess. I pull the knife from between the ears on my chest and sink it into my right eye. Colors explode. Many-faceted insects fly like diamonds from my eye in an army of knives that plunge into the fleeing and fortifying men. My eye sits on the tip of every blade, buried in their hearts, their lungs, their guts. My eyes stay alive inside them for centuries, watching them rot. Their bodies feed roots reaching into the future and the past, roots of the fungal mind-web living inside the earth.

Half-blind, I recognize the pox behind their masks. She came from the stars eons ago and inoculated our unborn planet. Creation spread like a contagion, a disease breeding many imposters and known by many names. Before the sixteenth century, physicians agreed all illness sprang from a single source. The pedigree of infection traced the disease of life to one fertile spore. Miasma poisoned the air, effluvium spread her symptoms. She was afforded proper worship until she bared her naked face at the close of the fourteenth century. Syphilis masqueraded through medieval Europe, and one hundred years of case histories quantified the Divine Pox: the smallest minds of the millennium replaced a deity with a diagnosis.

Her ancient roots grow through my multitude of eyes and the dead men on the ground and the wet floor of the house on Zuni Street. Where Nate cowers, a white oak spawns multiple trunks that erupt like sudden mushrooms in the damp house. Their gnarled arms communicate simultaneous narratives interlocking through hidden tree rings. History and the future connect within them like a chain linked from end to end in a circle. The clasp holds the chain together inside our warm flesh as a warning bell peals into the present day from fifteenth century Europe: Once we map the New World, Eden is impossible.

Before 1490, the fungal arms of white oak bloomed on all corners of the planet from shared roots like mad, insistent corals. Her trunks were felled, planed and sized, made ready to receive the pigment and prayer of craftsmen and artists. Layers of animal skin glue and gesso failed to obscure the living message carried in her veins. Medieval altarpieces hewn of her provenance intoxicated congregations by their mere presence. As time aged and desiccated the panels, curators harvested her sap as a sacramental balm, further depleting her potency. In the modern age, only the boldest heresy retains a trace.

The silence of the Inquisition on this matter proves their complicity with the argument embedded in the wood: a tree grows within a forest underneath the ground, an ancient fungal infection, a mind that mutates men into fruiting bodies of her will. "You are liars or fools who say I traveled to the Old World on the ships of Columbus or Cortez. I am endemic wherever there is life. Man is my vessel, and through him I will repopulate the stars. I am in the earth, but I am not of the earth."

"Baby," Nate says, scuffling through the carnage. "Babe, I can't understand you but I think we have to go."

Nate's voice again is gentle, tender, almost loving. But I don't need him to understand. I need him to hear. I need him to hurt me. I need him to hurt. I need him to come with me and stumble onto the sidewalk or into the abyss or out of this allegory and throw wide open the flat panels pinning us like a forgotten butterfly collection to the surface of things. I need him to help me come out from behind the glass.

"As above, so below," I decree. Nate pauses in his rush to escape the chaos. He peers at me in his shy way with his slurred smile. He's always been shy, started drinking young to manage his anxiety. Kept drinking to drown his father's voice calling him a fag because he liked art and fixed his sister's hair. Nate wanted to make his world more beautiful and ended up making it a slum. I met him when his life was done, when his stories were over-told and his clever ideas recycled, when his daughter refused to see him again and his ex-wives milked him dry. When I met him, Nate had nothing to offer me. I took it.

Nate holds my wrist and dips his finger in the little tub of gunk. He paints it onto my upper lip, dips again, and works on the lower with careful strokes until he's satisfied with the effect. His grip around my wrist leaves the watermark of his fingertips in my skin. His shy glance asks me if I recognize him: the hero playing the vagabond. I try to remain inscrutable. He kisses me. We drink the melting substance smashed between our lips with the seven tongues of a dragon he's slain and kept hidden in his pocket.

We lap up the gunk. I unzip his jeans and sheath him in the stuff. New parts spring forth in all directions. The receptive ones I plumb, spreading the substance and expanding organs that bloom between us like meaty flowers. I mount him, roots form, and the dead men around us stir. Nate's chasm widens. We plunge inside and eat the fruit.

In the New World, we find many strange and wondrous creatures. Birds of every color fly through air and water; rhinoceros, lion, and unicorn roam free upon the land. Men live like beasts, prized for their animal beauty and strength. Women suckle their young, unashamed. Exotic specimens both human and animal are brought to the auction block and deemed free of blemish by my European ancestors who trade their civilized microbial gifts of smallpox, measles and typhus in exchange for the New World's abundant crops. Mercenaries are imported, slaves are sold, Eden is exploited.

The great explorers, masters of navigating by the stars, surveyed their course according to the trajectory of reason. Those who donned the mask of syphilis in their old age deemed it the worthy price of enlightenment. Certainly, the stars would not lie.

I fuck Nate's voluptuous new orifice. It fucks me, and grips me, and sucks me dry. I see my face reflected in Nate's obsidian skin, doubled by the twin globes of his ass. The eyes that look back at me are feral and empty, diseased by a Tudor kiss.

‡

"You're home early."

I creep under the covers. It's three in the morning. "I didn't think you'd be here today."

"Yesterday."

"Sorry." I press into Eric, feeling his disgust.

Eric shifts, turns over, makes a barricade of sheets between our bodies. "We wrapped early. Extra pay." Eric makes military training films. It's not the creative work he craves, but it pays the bills. I've told him to quit. He's a painter by vocation. His brushes, paints and rolls of canvas clutter the back of the closet. Paint tubes harden. Brushes lose their hair. Eric says we can't waste money on studio space. I say use the living room. He says that's irresponsible, what would people think. I say who cares, you have to live and that's what it's for. He says well, we can't all just do what we want, can we? I say why not? At some point in the rhetorical mess, Eric goes deaf.

I destroy all chance of an alibi. I don't want one. "You got back yesterday last night or yesterday Monday?"

Eric sighs. "Today is Thursday."

"Oh. Right." I sit up and look at Eric in the red glow of ambient light from the twenty-four-hour diner across the street. "What have you been doing for two days? Why didn't you call?"

Eric doesn't move. His body is an inscrutable landscape in the near dark, his voice an empty echo. "What have I been doing? Why didn't I call? Are you prepared to have a serious conversation at this hour?"

"No. I mean, I'm not prepared, I'm just, you know, concerned. I'm sorry. What did you do all this time?"

"Looked for you."

"I'm sorry."

"Stop saying that."

"But I am. Why didn't you call?"

"Go to sleep."

Inside me, there's a cathedral in flames. Ergot dancers surround the spires, casting obscene shadows in the red-tinged light as an apocalypse cracks the sky open like a raw egg. The man beside me doesn't see the figures licking the walls or the glare on the ceiling. He doesn't acknowledge the dizzying altitude of young mountains aglow with black and red wildfire that eats the trees. He's impervious to their screams. He doesn't ask me where I've been.

Tonight I told Nate it was over. Again. It wasn't the first time and it won't be the last. I'd tell Eric the same if he'd hear me. I'm sick of being the middle panel of our triptych, an incomplete story if I lose either wing. I can't survive as a solitary point in history, a grey globe interred by redundant chastity, closed and colorless, endlessly enduring the inertia of time's static symmetry. I need to fall off the flat edge of the world and embrace our collective fate. I want to fall: fall into the pit, or fly into the clouds, or both. If Hell is a product of history, Eden is a relic of eternity. Opposites conjugate in a compositional destination that binds the three of us together. We're hinged by the navigational rivalry of derelict stars. When we open our wings to take flight, we reverse the Fall of Man. If the end result is a fantasy or a satire, at least we'll sabotage the sequential face of history as we sail into the fire.

Eric's body is a warm, rhythmic beast beside me. Asleep, there's no anger on his face, no suspicion or disdain. He walks in the garden, the paradise that never existed outside an older man's dream of Eve's fidelity. He ignores the swans with too many heads, the restless gaze of owls. I slough off Eric's cocoon of sheets, exposing his flesh to my fingers. He's muscular, but his surface has softened with age into something both firm and pliant. I caress the paradox of his back. He's mistaken about Eve. She's not demure. She cuts across antiquity to expose the Father of Man as an imposter. Eve doesn't look down out of modesty or fear. She looks down out of boredom and resignation. Adam isn't enough.

When Eve looks up, and always she must, the future rages like a newborn pestilence. Enlightenment ravages the populace. Time spirals outward. Eric breathes less deeply as I draw my hands across his skin. I reach between his strong legs and brush the head of his lust as it bucks. Something involuntary and joyful like this grows inside me too. Maybe this time we'll evolve. Maybe this time we'll make it work. I want Eric to have more than one head, more than one life, more than one chance for enlightenment. One life is not enough. I wake him by pressing him into me where I'm still wet. His eyes stay closed. I'm careful to keep silent.

We fit together too well. Our incongruities shock. We came west together seeking emotional gold. The new delighted us. At the Mercado on Zuni, we practiced our Spanish with lavishly rolled "R"s until I halted at the deli case. Pig heads lined up before me with eyeless sockets. They stared like the heads in the window of the retirement home, watching without seeing, like unstrung puffballs in a fairy ring forced out of their circle to concede to linear time. Reflected in the deli glass, my face was transposed with the face of a dead pig.

The glare of sunlight obliterated the image. "Be careful," Eric said. "You'll hurt your eyes." He touched my back. I jumped. Purple sunspots skewed my smile into a grimace.

Eric pulled back. He's been orbiting away ever since. The harder I reach for him, the further away he recedes. We make love rarely, without speaking or looking. In public, we're the portrait of a happy couple, but beneath our painted surface, the mute flesh of butchered animals holds a primal grudge. Our muscles remember every cut, our severed flesh sags, and our gouged eyes are blind. We wear masks of deception. We live behind glass.

We live until we die or mutate. Fungal hyphae network through both the soil below and the spatio-temporal heavens above. My body is an arm of the organism, inoculating Eric with spores of the disease that will transform us into a unified, animated host. We are destined for space exploration in the New World. We are bound for undying love. We are bound to Nate and the dead men on Zuni and the thinking underground forest that entangles us in her divine web. She rewards us with her sticky glory.

As we enter and exit one another, advancing and retreating, coupling and uncoupling, Eric grows louder, almost looking, almost shouting. I haven't heard him like this in ages, haven't felt him take me like this in so long that I forget all motivation apart from my body and its construct of lust. I feed him its sacrament. I'm not sure about the consequences or the price. I'm sure that at this moment we're in a place more holy than any terrestrial church. Take, eat, this is my body.

But what if my body eats him first?

‡

I'm drinking a complicated red with a smooth finish, tasting oak in the back of my throat. The syphilis bacterium is shaped like a corkscrew. The irony isn't lost on me. I wear the life-token of the many-named plague in the scars on my chest. With age, my body has become a symphony of scars. Textures, creases, enlarging follicles, sunspots and tan lines blur into swarthy meat. My skin sings of illness. The drinks don't blur things like they used to, but I'll let you buy them if you like. I'm waiting for a friend.

I drove from Wisconsin to Denver without a reservation last night. Some insane chemical GPS called me to the Mercury Club like the rest of this throng. It's been ten years. Everyone looks like they came here to meet a blind date, eyeing one another, wondering when the show starts. I guess I'm not the only one who felt the call. Perhaps you felt it too.

It's getting late and you, my newfound friend, have listened to my story of love exploited and lost. I hope you don't think less of me. A triptych is a trap. In traditional form, the imaginary timelines of theology and the confluence of themes bind each panel to the rest. As separate entities, significance is lost, context is infinite. Randomly cropped remnants persist as puzzles the future may never unlock. What happens between creation and apocalypse? Is the middle panel the subject or the object? What sensation survives between lovers when we reject the boredom of the story and its conveyance? A triptych is engineered to be stable and portable. You carry it on your back when it's closed. It's almost a funny thought: an altarpiece like a traveling salesman's display ready to be propped up and gawked at.

"You're a woman of mystery," you say.

I roll my eyes. "You don't know me."

"I've seen you play."

"A triptych enfolds the viewer the way I hold my cello, like a lover between my legs, like a mother giving birth to an ekphrasis. She's an instrument from the Age of Reason, a Renaissance girl. You think she's austere, but deep down she's as needy as the rest of us. She begs to be plucked and bowed and strummed."

You say, "Mother, I want the sun."

"Excuse me?"

"Ghosts. I'm also on the stage, in theater. I'm Oswald."

I ask, "Is this research for your role?"

You answer, "It's more than that. My role makes me wonder what the world might be without the burden of a dead patriarch on its back."

"It's like you can read my mind. How many father figures do I have to destroy to escape this allegory? I have a thing for artists, especially the ones who don't make any art. Why is that so common? Why do so many great men fear genius and fall prey to the mundane? Don't you agree that the sexual and aesthetic goal of life is unencumbered freedom?"

You start to speak with a soft inhalation, and then interrupt your own breath when an old man and his caregiver enter the club. Your body moves like an act of grace, vanishing to an adjacent table.

I recognize Nate right away. He ducks through the doorway. His wavering frame in a vintage blazer hasn't changed. Same precarious height and poor connection, like his head will float away from his feet any second in a cloud of cigarette smoke.

An older white guy accompanies Nate. He's shorter, disabled, and it's not until he leans over to peck my cheek that I realize he's not older, he's Eric. His body smells like sulfur.

Eric acclimates to the seat on my right side, his body unbending at the joints. Nate lilts into the seat on my left like liquid.

Nate's half-smile half-glance half-love expression molds his face into a permanent caricature of himself. Or maybe he's drunk. Of course he's drunk. Eric is stone sober and won't let up on the eye contact, the demanding veracity of his vision. He's an artist with no model, a painter with no canvas, a starving hawk. His eyes accuse me and excuse me from above. I'm not a person to him. I'm prey. I take his hand, and Nate's.

"I can't believe you're here. I didn't know you two…um," I say.

"Yeah," Nate offers. "Well, someone had to take care of him."

The violence in Eric's eyes belies his gentle tone of voice. "After you left, he kept coming by. I don't pretend to know what you do. I have always been supportive. As you can see, I needed assistance."

Nate does that thing where he makes a kissy noise sucking on his cigarette. I want to kick him every time he smokes a cigarette. He says, "Don't blame her, dude."

Eric's face looks like bitten fruit. His flesh is puckered and rotten. "This isn't easy for me. I'm not here to blame anyone. You didn't have to hide anything from me."

Nate says, "She was young."

Eric says, "You didn't have to lie. Why did you lie?"

Their hands feel like two different species. Nate's thin fingers seep away from my grip. He's got a drink and a cigarette to tend. Eric clasps my fret hand like a threat. I pull it away out of instinct. It's been my livelihood all these years.

Eric says, "You didn't tell me you were sick."

"I wasn't."

Eric doesn't hear me. Nate says, "It's my fault."

"I'm not talking to you," Eric snaps at Nate and then turns

back to me. His hand is still open, expectant. "I will always care about you."

Parallel conversations ebb and flow around the club with similar hushed intensity. Each table flickers, candle at the center, black and red décor absorbing ambient light. Faces in various stages of decay implore, debate and confess, a gallery of grotesque, unthinkable masks poised for a ceremony to start. You, my friend, my spy, solitary and silhouetted by the glow of your phone, wait attentively as the human narrative exhausts itself.

Eric's premise is all wrong. I speak to you as much as to him. "Do you want me to be a bird with its wings sliced off, a shark with its fins amputated for soup, sinking to the depths and dying of immobility?"

"Don't be sad," Nate says.

"Stay out of this," Eric says to Nate, and then to me: "I'm trying to forgive you."

Nate says, "Nothing to forgive. I'm making amends."

Eric's eyes flash. "Is that what you call it? Free rent and free food, probably peddling my meds. I should throw you back on the street."

"Don't talk to him like that," I say to Eric.

"Hey, hey, it's okay," Nate says. "I mean, it is what it is. Somebody's got to take care of him. I got this, baby." Nate's body flows in close to me while Eric's rigid posture of pain nails him upright in his seat.

"This is all very touching," Eric says from a distance. "Don't you feel any remorse?"

I'm not sure which one of us he's talking to but I'm ready to answer. "Time wasn't supposed to be so fucking linear. It was a gift. Something we shared. I saw us growing and moving together and burning what we left behind."

"That's why you poisoned me? As a gift?" Eric's voice isn't so gentle anymore. Heads turn.

"It's not poison. Look around you."

"I'm dying," Eric says.

Nate says, "The forest is dying."

Roots below and above are withered. Hyphae joining us

through the fungal network burn away in the glare of modernity. Called by the chemical signals of an ancient organism's death-throes, we're a poorly reconstructed triptych, an anachronism. Looking around this somber congregation, I can barely imagine these beings as the frolicking, fruiting bodies of our shared, toxic vision; pale, inverted and many-limbed; joyful, innocent and wanton as we combine into a heretical geometry, a blueprint of paradox, an illuminated neuro-script. Our bodies will reconfigure into a manic vessel, the spaceship *Paradisum Voluptatis.* She will carry us aloft into the New World.

I say, "When we leave, this will be a dead planet. We're gathered for lift-off."

"This is fun," Nate says.

"This is bullshit," says Eric. "Let's go."

Nate's eyes almost open all the way. Eric fights to extract himself from his chair. His face reddens with effort. "She's crazier than ever. This is pointless. Do you understand?" Eric turns to me. "You know you need help. There's a cure. Sometimes it works." He struggles against the confines of his body. I can infer from his movements the ineffable beauty of the multi-dimensional, asymmetrical being Eric refuses to become.

I make one last attempt to reach him. "The cure is killing you."

Standing, leaning, Eric catches his breath and shakes his head. "Bat-shit crazy bullshit." He hobbles away, relying on his cane.

"Babe, I gotta motor." Nate's up and ready to follow. He's about a foot taller than me. He gets in so close I have to look up to see him. He says, "Call me. Okay?"

"What do you mean? If you stay, you'll die like him."

"Aw, I knew you loved me best. I won't tell. Almost forgot. I brought you something." Nate hands me a plastic baggy with some tablets of various shapes inside. Lint from his pocket is stuck to the baggy and the plastic is crumpled from re-use. It's no longer transparent.

Nate crushes me into his chest, leans down and puts his lips in my hair. "You loved me best."

"I—"

He says, "Shh."

I loved the idea of the man more than the man himself. I've looked for him, mourned for him, and known him by the singing of my scars, by the seven tongues hidden in his filthy pocket. He leaves one of them with me, bitten and dry. He leaves.

My spy, my snake, my newest friend, you palm the baggy and take the seat across from me. You're welcome to take them both. You say: "The faces we wear in this world are masks." You have effete cheekbones and glorious skin, and eyes still clear and bright with the ignorant kindness of youth. I suspect you've led a privileged life. You speak in a way that is wise, yet you can't possibly know that I avoid mirrors lest I see in my reflection the face of a dead pig.

I answer you as honestly as I can. "Beneath our feet, god is dying. The disease of life demands the stars."

"Does it? You share some colloquy?" You shift your shoulders forward and say "colloquy" as if I know what the word means. Your eyes are full of light and aspiration. "Will you share with me?" you ask.

Old sources of the sacrament have dried up. The antibiotics of the twentieth century eradicated most of our kind, and collectors of medieval art no longer guard the sacred argument of the hallucinatory sap. The drug is legendary, and outside of our bodies, it is lost, lost. My radiant new friend, the world is ripe for a new plague, and you're burning with faith. Who am I to stop time in her tracks? Why, indeed, would the stars ever lie?

You are naked and gleam like quicksilver, as though impervious to time. I'm less naked than you, but no less monstrous standing on the frontier of disintegration. I know Creation is a plague. I know that when desire transforms into violence, I will participate in the drama.

"Aren't you a bit young for this scene?"

"That's not important," you lie to me. "You're beautiful."

"I don't know if you're ready for this. Maybe you should take some of those pills."

"I don't need that," you say.

"Are you sure?"

The congregation's culled to less than fifty. Outside, we assemble into forms indeterminate as animal or vegetable or rock. We enact pornographic tableau, an exploded model of a medieval simultaneous stage. The chain of time closes and locks. Mycelium weave our raw nerves as one tendril, pulsating with ancient and modern thought. In the city, polluted by artificial light, the stars have gone blind. Orifices able to give and receive chart a didactic course as they increase. We navigate by multiplicity. The *Paradisum Voluptatis* ascends to the night sky with the glory of a symphony, an armed battalion greater than the sum of her parts.

Your heart beats too fast, your muscles clench. I told you to take the pills. I turn you over and push your face into the earth, our foster mother. You spit in her dirt and murmur your lines, "The sun, the sun." I pull back from the warm knot of your colon and release its new trickle of blood. To soothe you, I whisper in your ear as you grow limbs, voices, eyes:

"I'm the flat color on oak, the pigment cracked by age. What harm can I do to you? My waters are pictures of water. My lust is a satire of lust. My church is a creature inside you, a spore that spreads when you dream. My church is a doctrine of deception, a mask of love and horror. You wear it when you dream. Your dream is a weapon of desire; your body is the fruit of my dreams. Your body is the fruit of syphilis."

I press you into a new shape. We rise.

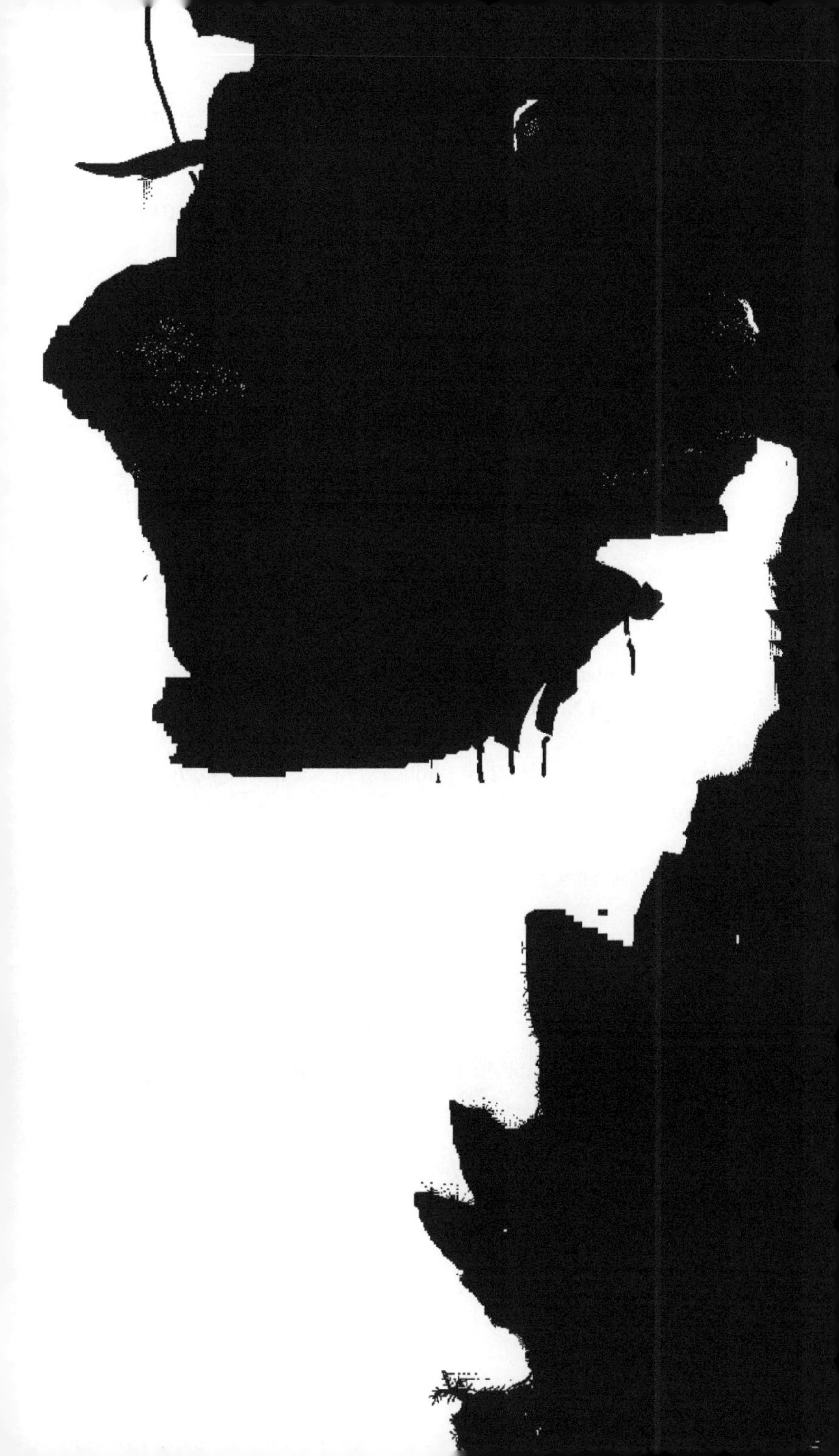

Previous Publication Acknowledgements

"Good Paper"- first published online in *Storgy Magazine*, 2019

"Offerings"- first published in Doorbells At Dusk from *Corpus Press*, 2018

"Blood Calumny"- first published in *Bodies Full of Burning: An Anthology of Menopause Themed Horror* from Sliced Up Press, 2021

"Aristotle's Lantern"- first published in *Stitched Lips: An Anthology of Horror* from Silenced Voices from Dragons Roost Press, 2021

"Rust Belt Requiescat"- first published in *Paranormal Contact: A Quiet Horror Confessional* from Cemetery Gates Media, 2021

"The Anatomical Christ"- first published in *The Big Book of Blasphemy* from Necro Press, 2019

"How To Fillet Angels"- first published in *Isolation Is Safety* from Filthy Loot, 2021

"The Buried King"- first published in *Black Telephone Magazine*, 2021

"Peaveman's Lament"- first published in *ProleSCARYet: Tales of Horror and Class Warfare* from Rad Flesh Press, 2021

"Swanmord"- first published in *Beautiful/Grotesque* from Weirdpunk Books, 2021

"Mr. Bones Puzzle Candy"- first published online in Horror Sleaze Trash, 2019

"The Revenge of Madeline Usher"- first published in *Not All Monsters*, 2020

"Mirror Grimoire"- first published in *Villains* from Iron Faerie Press, 2020

"The Object Of Your Desire Comes Closer"- first published in Synth #1, 2019

"Paradisum Voluptatis"- first published in *Honey & Sulphur* from CarrionBlue555, 2019; later reprinted in *Year's Best Hardcore Horror Volume 5: Going Global*, 2020

About The Author

Joe Koch writes literary horror and surrealist trash. A Shirley Jackson Award finalist, author of *The Wingspan of Severed Hands* and *The Couvade*, their short fiction appears in Year's Best Hardcore Horror, The Big Book of Blasphemy, Not All Monsters, and many other journals and anthologies devoted to speculative horror, weird fiction, and lyrical splatter. Joe has an MA in Contemplative Psychotherapy from Naropa University and a strong commitment to growing facial hair. Find Joe online at horrorsong.blog and on Twitter @horrorsong.

Lightning Source UK Ltd.
Milton Keynes UK
UKHW010628210422
401849UK00001B/180

9 781954 899056